ACCLAIM FOR
War Story

"*War Story*, Gwen Edelman's brilliant first novel, opens a new perspective on the history of the human heart; it's a tale of the Holocaust as it is lived not in memory, not in a library or in one of endless conferences, but in the real world, between generations, between lovers."
—Adam Zagajewski

"A train is rumbling through the 'endless fields of northern France' at the beginning of Gwen Edelman's accomplished first novel, about the love affair between an aging European playwright who has seen it all and a much younger American woman, who has seen almost nothing. . . . Within the short span of [a] journey, Ms. Edelman traces the somber and angry recollections of the young woman, whose encounter with the older man was not simply a love affair; it was a private lesson in the psychic and spiritual scars left by history. After him, another man would seem like a diluted experience, a fake. And that is the fierce hold that Joseph also has over Ms. Edelman's readers."
—Richard Bernstein, *The New York Times*

"[T]he spare language is seductive, as are Joseph and his horrific tales. With this resonant character, Edelman has convincingly tapped into the slow suffocation that follows the tragedy of war."
—*San Francisco Chronicle*

"A class act, spare, sardonic, fierce, and utterly unsentimental."
—A. Alvarez

continued . . .

Gwen Edelman lives in Paris. *War Story* is her first novel.

War Story

Gwen Edelman

RIVERHEAD BOOKS
New York

RIVERHEAD BOOKS
Published by The Berkley Publishing Group
A division of Penguin Putnam Inc.
375 Hudson Street
New York, New York 10014

Copyright © 2001 by Gwen Edelman
Readers guide copyright © 2002 by Penguin Putnam Inc.
Book design by Betty Jane Lew
Cover design © 2001 Royce M. Becker
Cover photograph © Roger Eaton/Photonica

First Riverhead hardcover edition: August 2001
First Riverhead trade paperback edition: August 2002
Riverhead trade paperback ISBN: 1-57322-939-3

Visit our website at www.penguinputnam.com

The Library of Congress has catalogued
the Riverhead hardcover edition as follows:

Edelman, Gwen.
War Story / Gwen Edelman.
p.   cm.
ISBN 1-57322-189-9
1. Holocaust, Jewish (1939–1945)—Fiction.
2. Reminiscing in old age—Fiction.   3. Holocaust survivors—
Fiction.   4. Funerals—Fiction.   5. Jews—Fiction.   I. Title.
PS3605.D45 W3   2001   2001019101
813'.6—dc21

Printed in the United States of America

10   9   8   7   6   5   4   3   2   1

War Story

Out the train window lie the endless fields of northern France, fallow, the spiky stubble dusted with frost. Everything is tinged with white, even the flat wintry sky and the pale face of the moon which rushes headlong through the white sky although it is only noon. How is it, wonders Kitty, peering out, that the moon keeps pace with them, always just above them, moving, moving as the train speeds through the frozen countryside. Chilly air seeps in beneath the window and Kitty pulls up the collar of her coat. Every so often they pass a small village, a cluster of houses and the sharp narrow steeple of an old church. The country makes me nervous, Joseph used to say. One night with the darkness and the baying of hounds and I'm ready to pack up and leave right away. You find little villages charming? Good. You can have them. Kitty hasn't seen him in ten years. Now she never will. Far away on a country lane a figure in high boots appears for a moment and fades out, too slow for the train which sweeps through like a cold wind.

All those years ago, he would rush ahead of her down the platform, his old battered suitcase bumping against his leg. Hurry, he would call out, almost running, we'll miss the train. His pace would speed up, she could hear him panting as he began to run. We can't miss the train. Hurry up. The train was nowhere near ready to leave. It stood there, empty of passengers, the conductor lolling on the quay. But Joseph climbed the steps breathlessly and rushed down the empty aisle to a seat. Settled next to her, he would pull out a large white handkerchief and wipe his moist forehead. We made it, he would say, trying to catch his breath, we made the train. And there they would sit, squeezed together on the seat and he would take her hand. Thank God, he would say, we made it. And Kitty would stare at the empty luggage racks, the undisturbed squares of white cloth pinned to the backs of the seats.

———

How could she understand this rush, having to arrive an hour early, the headlong flight down the platform, the sweaty palms, the damp forehead? Why should they miss the train? And if they did they would get the next one. There was always another train. You don't understand, do you? he would ask, turning toward her in the seat of maroon plush. No, she would say shaking her head, how can I? No, he agreed, you can't. Well never mind. Would you like an orange? He pulled one from his pocket. You know I don't like them. He put it back again and looked at his watch. Good, he said happily, we're in plenty of time. And they would sit together, all alone in the long train. Come in the bathroom darling, he would whisper. Let me make you a baby.

The train arrives in Amsterdam at 2:13. The funeral is at three. In a synagogue. When she knew him he wouldn't have dreamed of setting foot inside a synagogue. Yet he knew the prayers and one of his favorite jokes ended with the first lines of the kaddish, the prayer for the dead. Go to synagogue? he would ask her. What for? He doesn't hear me from where I am? Only in His own house? I don't believe it. Where were Abraham, Isaac, and Jacob when they called out to Him? Certainly not in a synagogue. Kitty studies the whorls of frost that have collected in the corners of the glass. Besides, he would add, He wouldn't let me in. I've slept with too many women.

How do people live with this interminable soil, wonders Kitty. She would feel buried alive. A tractor lies tipped at a precarious angle on a small embankment, its heavy black treads off the ground. Why has the farmer left it so far away? He will have to walk miles to reach it, thinks Kitty, but she knows nothing about the lives of farmers and perhaps there is another solution. Before I became a writer, Joseph used to brag, I worked in the fields. In the orange groves in Palestine after the war. Where do you think I got these shoulders from, these strong upper arms? Kitty would touch his upper arms lightly. I thought, she would say, that you got them from lifting so many women and carrying them off to bed. It's you I'd like to lift, he would say, never mind the others. And he would bend down and press his broad forehead against hers. I am listening to you think, he would say.

The conductor comes through and asks for her ticket. His dark mustache fills the space between mouth and nose and spreads out toward his cheeks as though he had been barbered in another century. Because she wants to keep him in front of her for another minute Kitty asks him when they will arrive in Amsterdam. Never, I hope, he says surprisingly. Why is that? Kitty wants to know. The mother-in-law's expected. She's blowing in with the snowstorm. It's already coming down in Amsterdam. We've had it over the radio. They're expecting a blizzard. Kitty has read that when the ground is frozen and cannot be dug up, the body must wait above ground. A gravedigger can break his shovel on frozen ground. . . . And burials? asks Kitty sharply. What's that, miss? replies the conductor. He punches her ticket and tips his hat.

With his wild crown of wavy hair, his heavy dark lidded eyes, obstinate chin and large chest, he attracted attention wherever he went. He had a magnetism that drew not only women, but men as well. He lorded it over waiters, he rapped impatiently at the windows at railroad stations, he treated cabdrivers imperiously. Though he had no money he always traveled first class and would not set foot in a bus or subway. His white hair stood out from his head, he radiated confidence. This was a man, one would have said, who knew his place in the world.

Nothing could have been further from the truth.

There was no place for us, he told her, not a place on earth that wanted us. And so he called out in restaurants and barged ahead in lines, and when he sneezed, as though he were playing in a Viennese operetta, everyone turned to look. Not so loud, Kitty would plead as he called out impatiently, the waiter will come in a moment. Poor darling, he would say looking at her with disdain. Are you suddenly a small mouse? Afraid to stir the dust? It's not that, she would protest. What then? You hypocrite, he would whisper, pressing his forehead against hers. Haven't you dreamed your whole life of escaping from tiresome rules?

Don't forget me, she used to say to him. Forget you, my darling? he would reply. How could I forget you? You are tattooed on my heart. But then his attention would wander, he would move into the past, absent himself. The electricity disappeared and he was no longer there.

The white winter sky is endless above the fields. The wonderful Dutch, he used to say, who reclaimed their land from the sea. The brave hardworking Dutch. Kitty likes the old Dutch paintings of this sky, this flat placid landscape. He wasn't interested. Shall I float in an old sentimental tale? he asked. My Holland is a different Holland. I'm not a sentimental dreamer like you. Don't frown my darling, he would say seeing her expression, taking her chin in his hand and kissing her. He would shake his head. So sensitive. How would you have survived the war? You better learn a little toughness.

Kitty winds her cashmere scarf around her neck. By the side of the window the aqua pleated curtain fans out like a skirt. Why are you going? Henri asked this morning, helping her on with her coat. She has lived with him for nine years. You don't still love him? She laid her head against his clean white shirt and closed her eyes and felt him lay her collar down flat. His fingers lifted up her hair. There's a casserole for you in the refrigerator, she told him, and a chocolate dessert. But what was it about him, he insisted, that was so fascinating? She stood up straight and began to button her coat. Nothing at all, she replied. I'll call you when I get to Amsterdam. He ran his hands quickly through bristly gray hair. I never could read his plays, he said irritably. Could you? So depressing. She went to turn out the chrome lamp over his desk. I'll be home tomorrow. He stood helplessly. I'll come down with you. No darling, it's light as a feather. He lifted the small leather bag and grimaced. It's heavy. What have you got in here? She took the bag from his hand. Don't be so curious. A book for the train. She kissed him quickly, a hand on his hip. He is always there, a fixed planet. Call me, he said with worried eyes. Kitty nodded. While Joseph was never in the same place twice.

When she went to the market with Joseph, he bought everything. Pounds of fruit, cheeses, vegetables, coffee, sausages, three loaves of bread. What are you doing? she would ask him. We can't eat all that in a month. You never know, he would reply, prodding a melon with his fingers, lifting it to his nose to smell its ripeness. Don't throw it out, he would say a week later as she stood above the garbage can with the soft spoiled fruit, the overripe cheeses, the two hardened loaves. I absolutely forbid you. But Joseph, she would plead, it's gone bad. Never mind. We can eat it anyway. Once there was no food to be had, he reminded her. You know nothing of that. But that was fifty years ago, she would say wearily. And there was a war on. If there was one, there can be another, he told her, taking the rancid-smelling box of cheese from her hand. Later when he went out for cigarettes, she threw it all out and put it out back to be collected.

The trolley passes and a cadaverous man in a short black jacket with gold buttons asks if she would like something. She studies the display of nuts and candies, the basket of croissants, the sandwiches in paper. The man waits expressionless, his face waxy, his pale blue eyes staring beyond his cart. Monsieur? Slowly he turns to her and inclines his bony head. Les biscuits au chocolat. His pale fingers pluck out the package and he hands it to her in slow motion. She munches on the cookie, like those she used to eat as a child. Against the low-leaning white sky a village flashes by, and in the distance a water tower the size of a child's toy. Joseph would come back from the snack bar armed with boxes of cookies and candies, sandwiches, chips. My God, she would cry in alarm, we can't eat all that. What if there is an emergency? he wanted to know. We won't starve. What emergency? Anything can happen, he told her, holding out a box of chocolate cookies. Better to be prepared. She looked at the candy bars in her lap and shook her head. He kissed her then, pulling her chin around to him. I know better, he murmured.

It was in a bookstore in New York that she first saw Joseph. A dim old-fashioned shop paneled in dark wood, silent in the heat of summer. She sat hunched on a three-legged stool in the corner of a small alcove, reading. "The woman was wearing a kimono and the long skirts trailed on the wooden floor." Kitty bent over the book. But soon she became aware of someone breathing, and putting her finger on the page to mark her place, she looked up. In the doorway stood an older man with broad shoulders, a belly, and unruly white hair, looking at her out of heavy-lidded eyes. I thought you looked Polish, she told him later. Or Israeli. The man seemed to be staring at her legs. And her breasts. Kitty pressed her legs together and held the book up in front of her blouse. He wore baggy corduroy pants. And a blue shirt. A button was unbuttoned over his belly and she caught a glimpse of white. He stared fixedly at her.

The air was heavy and the spines of the books muted with dust. Well, asked Kitty at last to break the silence, what is it? I want to know, he said slowly, although he could easily see the title, what it is you're reading. He had a guttural accent she could not identify. Why do you ask me when you can read it yourself? I'm making conversation. Kitty smiled. All right, she conceded. What is it about? It's about a man who goes to visit a geisha. And? he asked. What happens with this man and his geisha?

His forehead was covered in perspiration from the heat of the small room. The man from Tokyo has not seen the geisha in a year, has forgotten to send the dance instructions he promised her. The woman tries to smile behind her white powder but suddenly her face collapses and her eyes fill with tears. She loves him more than he loves her, said Kitty out loud, the book resting on her lap. The man shrugged. That often happens. And then? Does she sing to him plucking a ukulele or do they go right to bed? Kitty looked at him, hesitant. Through the gap in his

shirt, she saw the white sliver of undershirt. They go right
to bed, she said at last.

Later he would say: I met you in a whorehouse. Or was it at
an all-night poker game. I met you in a bookstore, Kitty
would remind him. In a bookstore? Impossible. I never set
foot in bookstores. You're the one who likes to read, not me.
You're the one who told me you spent your childhood in an
apple tree, hidden by leaves, turning the pages. One leafy
afternoon . . . you told me. Do you remember? Kitty nodded. But I still met you in a bookstore. I was seated in the
corner on a three-legged stool. Reading a book. What nonsense. I found you in a bordello. You were only fourteen.
Thirty-two. Then you lied about your age, you strumpet.
How can I have anything to do with you? You monster, she
murmured, tugging at his hair. He had always to find the
better story.

They pass through a tunnel and the roar of the engine is
thrown back on them. Against the darkened window Kitty
sees the face of a man somewhere ahead of her, the collar
of his coat turned up. His hair is dark and he has narrow

almond eyes like a Tartar. There is something catlike about him. Kitty, unseen, stares. He is peeling an orange, tearing off the dimpled orange skin with ungloved fingers. He works slowly and carefully. Kitty watches his long fingers. After a moment he looks up and sees her reflection. He lifts his eyebrows in a kind of query. And then with a sucking sound and a sudden pale blinding light, they emerge from the tunnel and the frozen fields begin again. Kitty looks up the aisle but from where she is sitting she cannot see him. Only his reflection. Joseph was sixty when she met him. And she was thirty-two. But she might have been fourteen, the way she behaved with him at first.

Kitty had bought the book about the geisha and the man from Tokyo and gone out into the heat of the afternoon with the man to have a coffee. The leaves hung limply on the trees, the pavement shimmered with humidity. Kitty's blouse clung to her. A bicycle with one wheel removed had been left leaning against a railing. As they walked in silence his hip touched hers. I don't know, said Kitty hanging back at the door to the coffee shop, pulling at her blouse. What a child you are, he said. What can happen to you in a well-lit coffee shop in the middle of the day? He grabbed her elbow and pulled her inside. The worst is to hesitate. While you hesitate, the bomb goes off. Or they grab you off the street. Where is that? asked Kitty. Never mind, he replied and indicated a booth.

Greek waiters with shiny black hair and limp white nylon shirts took orders, shouting them out in Greek at the small window to the kitchen. Kitty slid into the red leatherette booth. Well, he began, seated across from her, isn't it about time? Don't you want to tell me your name? He looked at her ironically. My name, she replied politely, is Kitty. Kitty? he asked in disbelief, wiping his forehead with a large white handkerchief. Like a little cat? What kind of parents give their child a name like that? It's a provocation to all men. Under his arms and in patches across his chest, his blue shirt was dark with perspiration. What about you? asked Kitty. Joseph. My father wanted to call me Friedrich after Friedrich the Great. But for once my mother prevailed and I was called Joseph. After the biblical Joseph, according to my mother. After our dear departed Emperor Franz Joseph according to my father. Kitty leaned forward. Where are you from? she asked. Not so fast my darling, he replied, pulling out the large white handkerchief. That is a long story. Hey, he called out, raising his arm to attract the waiter, two coffees. He has no manners, thought Kitty with dismay.

The waiter set down two cups of coffee on the Formica tabletop and pushed the sugar bowl toward them. Joseph's white hair rose up from his forehead like a prophet. He is at least twenty-five years older than me, thought Kitty. There were creases at the corners of his eyes, networks of tiny lines. Yet his eyes were clear as he studied her. But where were you born? insisted Kitty. I was born in Vienna. He drank his coffee black, his square finger pressed into the loop of the handle. But I did not stay long. It doesn't sound like a Viennese accent, said Kitty, her eyes on his long thin mouth. It's not. On top is piled Dutch and Hebrew and English, even some Russian. Kitty eyed him with awe. When did you leave Vienna? You are very persistent, he remarked. Are you a social worker? Kitty smiled. Never mind, she said. You don't have to tell me. She emptied two packets of sugar into her coffee and stirred it slowly. Well in that case, he replied, I will. She looked up, waiting. I left Vienna when I was eleven. Why did you leave? You look so nice, he said, with your long hair and your green eyes. And then it turns out that you are the Grand Inquisitor. All right, she said lightly, never mind. Again never mind.

He took hold of her hand and spread out her fingers against his palm. Look what beautiful hands you have, he said softly. So white and so graceful. They should be sculpted in white marble. I left because I felt like a change. No, really. Really? I was in the mood for a vacation. It was 1938, a good year for vacations. She felt the warmth of his broad palm against her fingers. When she looked up, his dark gaze was on her. She took her hand away and lifted her cup. He looked down and sucking in his stomach, buttoned the button. She watched him. And he saw how she watched. It won't be long, he said.

He took her by the hand and led her to the hotel where he lived, half a block away. The great brick pile rose twelve stories, its facade dotted with black wrought-iron balconies. The paint on the balconies was chipped, the long maroon awning that said Hotel Stuyvesant was faded and torn. A hotel, he told her squeezing her hand, for madmen and artists. On the fifth floor a man composes for his giant turtles. On the tenth floor lives a German transvestite.

Leon Tucher on the eleventh plays the tuba and the pic-colo, in order, he says, that I may understand how we are gigantic and infinitesimal. The actress Damiana lives up-stairs and dresses in full costume whether she is going on-stage or not. Here, he said, leading her through a dark lobby hung with paintings, is where I am at home. A mad-man among madmen. Are you really a madman? asked Kitty letting go of his hand. Who is not? he asked and led her to the elevator past a small man with an eyeshade who sat behind the desk reading a creased newspaper.

That first time, that first afternoon, all those years ago. The white shutters closed against the afternoon light. In the liv-ing room the floors were bare, the sagging sofa draped with an old bedspread, stacks of books piled haphazardly against the blank peeling walls. It was as though no one lived there. Even the desk in the corner with the typewriter on it looked as though it hadn't been used in a long time. The surfaces were furred with dust. He watched her. One day, he said, I will get a maid in here. She nodded, walking quickly through the room. Sit, he ordered her, pointing to the long kitchen table. Here, she understood, was where he lived. The wood had been scarred with innumerable ciga-rette burns. A chipped plate of cold cuts and a plastic sausage of liverwurst had been set out beside a loaf of dark bread whose crumbs were scattered over the table. It was always like that. They would sit across from each other. A bottle of schnapps between them, or the teapot with faded circus scenes, or the copper coffeepot he had brought back from Israel. The little gold metal box stuffed with loose tobacco lay open and the packet of thin white sheets of rolling paper nearby. Now, he said, putting on the kettle, you will learn what real coffee is. What they serve in this country is thin and tasteless and brings no happiness. Drink my coffee and your troubles will be behind you.

On the wall beside the table old postcards, the cellophane yellowed, were pinned up with no space between them. Decades of postcards. Blue sea, donkeys, gothic cathedrals, long sandy beaches, an Amazon Indian painted with red clay, sunrise in Jerusalem. A lamp with a torn shade stood on the table and propped against the base of the lamp were more postcards. You could open a shop, said Kitty. He followed her gaze. Yes darling. And you'll sell. From a cupboard whose door hung open on sagging hinges, he pulled out a bag of coffee. She saw into the shelves where boxes were stacked one on top of the other in disorder. From one box a small mound of tea had escaped, from another yellow macaroni had spilled onto the shelf. In her parents' house, utter neatness reigned. Nothing was out of place, not a flake or a leaf. This was another world.

She studied his broad shoulders, his neck thick as a bull's as he poured the boiling water through the coffee. He waited reverently, still holding the kettle. Now. Two minutes. And then you will see my angel. This is what women love me for. My coffee. Kitty shrugged. He poured it out proudly. Taste it. No, she had said stiffly, it's too hot. Don't be jealous, he murmured. You've only just met me.

He sat down heavily at the table and taking off his shoes slipped on backless yellow Moroccan slippers. So what is it you want to know? he asked her. Kitty inspected the bread. About leaving Vienna. Under the table he took his foot out of the slipper and ran a stockinged foot up her calf. Stop, she complained. I want to hear. His foot traveled up farther. Drink your coffee, he said. He watched her raise the chipped cup to her lips. Well? he asked. Delicious, she answered politely. Good, he said. What did I tell you? He opened the top button of his shirt and she saw the curly white hair. He scratched unconcernedly. I left on a train filled with dark-eyed children, he said. Is that what you want to know? In November of 1938. I was eleven. Kitty nodded. We stayed up all night playing as the whistle shrieked in the night and the train took the curves. He pulled shreds of tobacco from the metal box and laid them in the small white square of paper. I had a little case. My mother had forgotten to pack my socks. And for this I could not forgive her. The smoke rose from his cigarette. Drink, he said to her. Don't let it get cold. He poured out more coffee into his cup.

The next morning at the Amsterdam station we stood together with name tags hung around our necks, clutching our little bags, and heard a guttural language we could not understand coming over the loudspeakers. I remember as we stood there, a dwarf walked by. He was smaller than we were, with a large hump, and he wore a black-and-white-checked suit and a felt hat with a feather which could have been Viennese. His face, when he got closer, was that of an old man, deeply wrinkled, with black eyes and a sharp very large beak of a nose that belonged on a full-sized man. We smiled at him, happy to see someone as small as we were beneath the soaring glass roof of an unknown station. He looked like a figure out of the books that had been read to us at home. Joseph spread a thick slice of bread with liverwurst and held it out to her. Take it, he instructed her, I don't want you to starve. He stopped in front of us children and pulling on his nose, he made a sound like a duck. And then he went on his way. Soon, we were claimed by those nice Dutch families who had agreed to take us in for a while. I learned Dutch in three months. In the family that took me in, there was a girl of thirteen. Hetty. I used to open the door when she was in the bath and watch her.

He got up and came around to her. Enough stories, he said quietly. He lifted her up and took her in his arms. No, said Kitty craning her neck away from him, I can't. No? Why can't you? She pulled away from him but he gripped her shoulders and kissed her. His mouth was warm and smelled of tobacco. She leaned into him, nearly collapsing, her legs faltering. He had had to hold her up. Look how you want me, he said to her, his hand already under her blouse. Wait, she said breathlessly, her cheeks flushed, pressing against his chest, trying to recapture his

fingers which were pulling at her nipple. But he was
pulling off her shirt and she felt something unravel in her
as, pressed up against him, he led her toward the bedroom.

That first afternoon, the bedroom dim behind closed shutters, he turned on a lamp and the room was suffused with
red light. I don't know, she had said, wavering. What don't
you know? he asked. The room was empty except for the
wide unmade bed covered in cresting white sheets. He began to unbutton her blouse and she grasped his hands.
Don't stop me, he told her and took her hands away. She
felt his mouth on her neck. For a moment she thought the
red light was blinking, but it was her eyelids blinking open
and shut. He was unfastening her skirt, pulling down her
panties until she stood naked before him, her flesh bathed
in the red light. He licked beneath her arms. She leaned
down to unstrap her high-heeled sandals but he stopped
her. A woman, he told her, must always keep something
on. Aren't you going to undress? she asked him. Everything in its own time, he murmured as he eased her back
onto the wide bed. Look what your belt buckle did, she
complained, showing him the red mark on her belly. He
knelt and kissed her there and then he undressed, letting

his clothes drop to the floor. He stood before her, broad-shouldered, his belly thrust forward, erect. She reached out her arms for him. Put your hand between your legs darling, he ordered her. I want to see you. Kitty hesitated. Go on, he encouraged her. She nodded, opening her legs, lifting her hand from the tangle of sheets.

So, thought Kitty, watching the frost-covered stubble of the fields, he would be buried in Amsterdam. Not in London or New York or Paris or Tel Aviv where he had lived after the war. But in Amsterdam which he could never forget. The Jewish Quarter is gone. Never mind, he told her, I never lived there anyway. He went back every year for forty-eight hours. That's enough, he told her. I breathe the air. I see the trees, their delicate branches reflected in the water of the canals. I go to the old cafes and see if anyone is still alive. But even those who are alive have gone away. It doesn't matter. I sit in a brown cafe and order a glass of genever, I speak Dutch to anyone I manage to engage in conversation, I unfold a Dutch paper, and strangely enough I am happy. Amsterdam was so clean then. In the morning you saw the solid Dutch housewives on their hands and knees washing the steps. It was them I thought of when I first learned to masturbate. Good decent women with their large bottoms pressing against the flowered material of their dress.

There was a time when she couldn't be without Joseph for half a day, when she ran to the Hotel Stuyvesant, walked quickly through the dark lobby, and stood before the elevator, pressing the button again and again, watching the floor numbers crawl by. And then the doors would slide open and she would step into that small fluorescent-lit box and rise up and up, her cheeks flushed, tapping her foot impatiently until the ninth floor. She would hurry down the long hallway and stop before his door, already breathless. When she rang the doorbell, at first there was silence. And then from inside she would hear the swishing sound of his flattened yellow leather Moroccan slippers across the wooden floor, coming closer and closer as she touched her hair, her lips, clutching her bag. She had worn black garters for him. And no panties. Flushed, she waited for him to come. And then she would hear the locks open and he would be standing before her. You look, he would say, as though you've been running for a train. With an abrupt movement of her shoulder she would turn and start to walk away. With a smile, he would grab her arm and pull her back in, closing the door. You devil, he would whisper. Why do you do this to me? I followed you, she told him later, as though you were the Pied Piper of Hamelin. He ruffled her hair. For you, my darling, I was.

Without a word they began pulling off their clothes. They lay strewn the length of the hall and across the living room. Worse than refugees, he would say, lifting her up high in celebration. The suitcases were so heavy that as they walked along the road, they began parting with their belongings, one thing after another. The routes they took were littered with discarded clothes. Just like us, my angel, he said, opening her legs.

Kitty lay in his arms, her eyes half closed. The white shutters were closed and the room lay in dimness. I was thinking, she said turning toward him. The story you told me about leaving Vienna. You should write about it. He began to laugh. What is it? she asked, uncomfortable. He rose up on one elbow and took her hand, his cheeks flushed with mirth. I have, my darling. Again and again

and again. That's all I do. You're a writer? Of course I'm a
writer. Have you heard of Joseph Kruger? My God, said
Kitty softly, pulling the sheet up over her shoulder, I
didn't know. Why didn't you tell me? What would it have
changed? Would you have done things differently? Made
love a different way? Cried out louder? Or softer? Kitty
shook her head. I feel like an idiot. No need darling, no
need. He took her breast in his hand. Shall we do it again?
Now that you know who I am. She looked over at him
and smiled. You're still the same. He shook his head, his
cheek creased from the sheets. What madness. Of course
I'm still the same.

Have you read my books, my plays? Kitty shook her
head. Not yet. Then your education is not complete.
Never mind. Now you'll read them. Whenever a woman
sleeps with a writer, she wants to read his books right
away, to go deeper, she thinks, than she has gone in bed.
Then, she reasons, I will understand my lover. But does
she? What he conceals in bed, he also conceals in his
books. Not necessarily, said Kitty carefully. He shows
more than he thinks. Who are you, he asked darkly, the
expert? Kitty shrugged. I know something about books.
Not a writer, I hope, he said, watching her. I want to be,

said Kitty looking away. Well well, he said. Then you've come to the right place.

The first book he gave her was *The Collected Plays*. You look so arrogant, she said peering at the jacket photo. Yes, he said with satisfaction, leaning over her, I do. And shall I tell you why? He took the book from her and stared into his own image. The Nazis thought the way to recognize a Jew is by the size of his nose. Nothing could be further from the truth. It's all in the eyes. You had only to look at the fearful cringing look in the eyes of the Jews and you knew right away what was what. But, he went on, his voice rising, I was cleverer than that. For months I stood in front of the bathroom mirror, willing my eyes to look confident, even contemptuous. No more Jewish eyes. He closed the book and Kitty looked up at him. The only thing is, once the war was over, I couldn't change back. It had stuck. I will tell you the truth, my sweetheart. I found it difficult to go back to being a Jew. He took up a pen. What is your last name? Jacobs, she told him. He looked at her in surprise. Jewish? I wouldn't have guessed. And I am the expert. Well well. That makes two of us. He opened the book and wrote: For Kitty Jacobs, the little cat. Love is lighter than we think. Joseph Kruger. She has it still. With all the others he signed for her. They are tucked behind other books on her bookshelf. She has not looked at them in years. Not since Kafka . . . they wrote about him. Not since Stalin, she used to say when she was angry with him. And at the end she was angry with him all the time.

Out of the three books he wrote, three of them are set in Amsterdam. The man who hid in a glue factory. The man who turned into a fish and hid beneath the water of the canal. The man who hid with the whores. I came from a Zionist family, he told Kitty. We were supposed to long for Palestine above all other places on earth. Happiness was to finally reach the Holy Land. But the Holy Land was too hot and too dry. And who needs palm trees? It was Amsterdam that I really loved. Have you been there? Seen the narrow canals with the arched bridges? Walked to the end of the Brewers Canal and seen the sea open up before you? Eaten fresh herring washed down with genever? And those Dutch girls with their milky lips. What a paradise.

———

Aimlessly, Kitty stirred what was left of her coffee. So terrible, she said. Joseph looked at her angrily, his hand at the opening of his striped bathrobe. Terrible? What was terrible? You don't understand. I wanted to leave Vienna. He let his cup clatter noisily into the saucer. Do you think they kicked me out? he said in a fury. Not at all. I wanted to leave. No one forced me to leave. His voice rose. You have no idea how happy I was. I didn't have to go to school. No parents. Girls everywhere. It was a holiday. Can you understand that? A holiday. All that was missing was a striped beach umbrella. And even that was there if you wanted it. I left of my own free will, he repeated stubbornly. No one kicked me out. Kitty sucked on her spoon. His mouth was set, his eyes dark. No one.

Do you think I am what I appear to be? he used to ask her. I am an actor, my darling, always playing a role. Don't forget that I studied at the Max Reinhardt School in Vienna after the war. I am a flea and a lion. Sometimes both at the same time. A tightrope walker balancing on a rope the width of a hair. You want to leave your proper home and come along for a few hours, a few days? You want to be caught up in madness. Is that it? He leaned down and pressed his forehead against hers. Inside, he whispered, his lips against hers, I am as small as a hazelnut hiding behind a leaf. Kitty laughed in surprise. I don't believe you! Smaller than a fly's ear. Kitty drew back to look at him. But into his eyes had come a look of icy arrogance and he turned away.

He poured out two small glasses of schnapps. My Dutch foster parents were good stolid predictable burghers. But I didn't hold it against them. Everything according to rule and regulation, everything at its appointed time. This is why when the orders came they knew just how to follow. He was short and balding with moist dark eyes which he always wiped when he blew his nose, as though cleaning up involved all the features of the face, not just one. He left like clockwork each morning at eight-thirty to go to the insurance company where he sorted papers for a living. Put his hat on his head and walked down the steps in his freshly shined shoes. Until this evening, he never failed to say. After work he sat in the armchair with the green fringe and read the paper, clicking his tongue. No good, he would say, shaking his head, no good, until we all began imitating him.

One night, to my great surprise, he put down the paper and told me he would teach me how to make an egg disappear. He must have taught his trick to the Germans because no sooner were they around than all the eggs disappeared. And not only eggs. He was surprised how quickly I learned. Said I was a natural magician. While my foster mother called out to me from the kitchen to please return the egg. She lectured me on staying clean and saying my prayers. She checked to see that I had washed and made me change my underwear. Cleanliness was for her the highest good. She kept her kitchen spotless, scrubbed and polished the floors, and aired the bedding every week. They doted on little Hetty and when they discovered me in the bath with her (I no longer stood at the door), all hell broke loose. They did everything but threaten to send me back to Austria. Still, they weren't too bad. And Hetty. She liked to take imaginary trips, particularly later when she couldn't leave the house. She looked too Jewish with her soulful eyes and dark curly hair. China, she would say. We are going to

China. And together we crossed the desert on camels and rode down the Yangtze River on a royal barge, and traveled on the Great Wall by carriage. She was a Chinese princess and I was the Emperor's son who had fallen in love with her. Little nightingale, she wanted me to call her, and kiss her hand. Not more. Not then anyway. Although I certainly tried. They weren't too bad really. He drank back his schnapps and poured another one. You don't drink? He pushed the glass toward her. Drink my angel, it's good for the soul.

Kitty coughed, her eyes watering. Strong, she said. What happened to them? What happened to who? he asked. To your foster family? He laid a seam of tobacco on a square of paper. What happened to them? They went away. Kitty imagined a trip to the sea, or to France.

Joseph was always in his striped bathrobe, his feet stuck into his Moroccan slippers. Seated at his kitchen table, rolling a cigarette. The light was always dim, the shutters fastened. Don't you ever go out? she would ask him. When I have to, he would reply. But we're cozy here, aren't we, my angel? Or would you rather we go and sit at Grand

Central Station? He slathered a slice of bread with goose fat. The night before the German invasion of the Netherlands, I went in while Hetty was in the bath. I ordered her to stand up and I put my fingers up between her wet legs. She was so thin but between her legs it felt soft. She started to cry out but I shook my head warningly and she grew quiet. The next day, when the tanks rolled in and the streets were filled with black uniforms, I knew that I and I alone was responsible for this catastrophe. Hadn't I put my fingers in a forbidden place? And this is how God was punishing me. I had proof of what I had always heard—that God's justice is swift.

As time went on Hetty got thinner and thinner. She was nervous all the time. She could no longer go to school and she sat indoors curled up in a chair, not like a cat, more like a snail. I tried to make her laugh, but nothing was funny to her anymore. Her sad dark eyes got larger and larger in her small white face. I tried to stroke her hand. I told her my best jokes. Nothing worked. One day I found her at the open window looking down. I want to jump, she told me matter-of-factly and when she half turned to look at me her nostrils were pinched and her face floury. Hetty, let's go to China, I proposed. You will ride on the back of a fire-breathing dragon, dressed in flowing silks and ropes of pearls. You will wear a cape made from the feathers of a thousand peacocks. Everyone will bow down as you pass because you are the Empress, the most beautiful and most powerful person in the land. I will be beside you with flaming swords in each hand to protect you. . . . But for once Hetty did not want to go to China. Let me jump, she said quietly. She was fifteen.

Come on darling, let's go to bed. Wait, said Kitty, we just got out. But I'm ready for it again. Just a minute, let me have something to eat. He got up and went to the cupboard and took out half a loaf of bread and a small jar of herring. He pulled out a board and brushed off the crumbs. Let me serve you, he said. He took up a bread knife and sliced into the dense dark bread. Dark bread with herring. What could be better? She looked at the open sandwich doubtfully. Go on, he urged her. Be a good Jew. She took a bite and smiled at him. You like that? he asked softly and pinched her cheek. Tastes good my sweetheart? I don't know what it is, he murmured. I can't keep my hands off you. Because I'm younger, ventured Kitty. Ho ho, he replied, do you know how many younger women I've had? I don't care, said Kitty defiantly.

He smiled at her. Darling, you're even younger than I thought.

He took her in his arms and licked at the crumbs at the corners of her mouth. Black bread, herring, schnapps, he murmured. You smell like Vilna, you smell like Lublin, you smell like Czernowitz. What don't you smell like. He smiled at her. What would your respectable parents say? He pushed her hair back from her forehead. Shall we run away together? I'll teach you German. Real Viennese Jewish German. I'll start again, he said excitedly. I'll write plays again. They'll open at the Burgtheater and I'll shave every day and meet the press, just like I used to do. What do you think? Shall we do it my sweetheart? Start again? Kitty kissed him eagerly. His arms dropped. What is it? she asked. What's wrong? It's a fantasy, he cried, what else would it be. Does life begin again? Does the past float off like a barge down a fog-shrouded river? Please. I should know. Maybe you could begin again, said Kitty. Are you crazy? he said heavily. There is no escape. Like some kind of beetle dragging three times its weight we all carry our pasts strapped on our backs. No putting it down. No stopping at an inn and laying down the burden for a night. He sat at the table and poured out a drink. His white hair was as dry as leaves. His eyelids sagged. Kitty sat down across from him. At the sides of his eyes was a weave of small lines. She waited. After a while he reached across and took her hand in his. Never mind darling, he said. We're alive, aren't we?

What time is it? asked Kitty turning back the cuffs of her kimono. This I couldn't tell you, replied Joseph. If my parents could see me, she went on, examining the coffee stain on the cuff, holed up in here, coffee stains on my robe, my hair a rat's nest. What a good girl you are, he said. You know nothing of life. She picked at a stain. I had a respectable job. I edited manuscripts for a publisher. Well you were lucky to get out from all that dust, he remarked. I left because I wanted to write. And? And then I sat at my desk and stared into space and the words didn't come. He shrugged. A writer writes. When he can, she said quietly.

What kind of Jews are they, your parents? Kitty thought for a moment. Unobtrusive ones. They don't say they aren't. But they don't say they are either. I didn't know any Jews until I left home. Except for the ones in books. My parents never spoke about the past. And because they wouldn't speak of it, it was the only thing that interested me. She leaned toward him. I have read about the war, she said. I know what happened. Do you? he asked ironically. She flushed. Never mind my sweetheart. You are the sexiest girl I know. And I have known a lot of them. I wanted to know about the war, said Kitty slowly, because it seemed to me that I belonged with those dark-eyed Jews. I don't mean that I wanted to share in their destruction, she added quickly. It was just that my true home seemed to be with them. Here my parents had really arrived, they thought, with a great big lawn and large white colonial with black shutters. And all I could dream about was the dark-eyed Jews sitting down to a meal in Prague. Or Berlin. Or Budapest. They would spot me sitting out on the lawn, reading a book about the war. The daffodils would be out and the oaks spreading their great leafy branches. What's the matter with you, they would say, nearly distraught, why do you want to read about all that? And I felt that if they could, they would have grabbed the book away from me. But that would have been un-American. I lived in those books. Joseph looked at her appraisingly. And now perhaps, you want to live in this one.

My mother would ring a little silver bell and we would wait in silence until Ruby came in, her apron gleaming white over her black uniform, her black skin smooth and mysterious. There was so much silence in those days. No one talked about what they were thinking. Ruby brought in the platter and took it back out. And then suddenly my mother would start in brightly: Saw old Mrs. Thomas today. And I would chew slowly on my roast beef. . . . Kitty laughed mirthlessly. The boredom. You have no idea. So what will you write about? asked Joseph blowing out smoke rings. Silence at the family table? That won't sell many copies.

My father polished his elegant brown leather shoes every night until they gleamed. My mother wore a lacy bedjacket and sat up in bed for half an hour reading an English detective story before she turned off the light. Marriage looked pretty dull to me. Joseph laughed mirthlessly. Worse than that, he said. And yet, said Kitty faintly, turning away, somehow I dreamed of it. But a wilder version. A freer version. My sweetheart, said Joseph pityingly, marriage is neither wild nor free. That is a young girl's fantasy. I know something about it. I was married twice. A madness without end. I learned my lesson.

———

Kitty's parents had never taken her to a synagogue. They wanted to leave all that behind them. Let's go once, Kitty suggested when she was little, just to see what it's like. Her father patted her head. No need, he said with a smile, you're better off without it. But just let me peer inside, she said. I want to see who's there. Instead they took her on the Freedom Trail, to Boston and Philadelphia to see cracked bells and old Quaker congregations and the dark-timbered house of Paul Revere. Here the Declaration of Independence was signed, her father said with excite-ment, showing her the document beneath glass. But the old parchment meant nothing to her and when they got out she stared up at the blue sky shirred with white clouds like fish scales and wondered who she would have been if she had been born in faraway Europe before the war.

She looked into Joseph's eyes and a kind of peace came to her. He looked like a Middle Eastern potentate in his striped satin robe, pouring out the coffee, his chest thrust out. She sat on his lap. Joseph, she said slowly, tugging at his ear, you mustn't leave me. My darling, he replied, if life has taught me one thing it is that one must be ready to leave at the drop of a hat. That was then, said Kitty. He shook his head. What has changed?

It is under this same earth, Kitty thinks, staring out the train window, that we are all buried. This crumbly dark soil, where we will lie. She thinks of her own death. If he can die, so can she. And with us everything goes. And love? Is that interred with our bones? You're far too sentimental, he used to scoff. Your descriptions of the moon and of love. A writer must be cool and detached. He would button the shirt button over his belly which always came unbuttoned. Like me. When I write I'm as cool as anything. No sentiment at all.

They were all slim volumes, his hallucinatory books about the war. No one could take more. In his hands the world was turned upside down and inside out. In the ferocity of his vision, there was no light that had not been snuffed out. It was a picnic, he would say about the war, a funfair. Better than the Prater where I went when I was a child. Better than the man who bit the heads off the chickens. Better than the fat lady, the magician, and the man who sold dirty postcards put together. You want to be a writer, he said to her mockingly. What will you write about, love and flowers? Maybe, said Kitty, playing with a strand of her hair. Or maybe I will write about you. Write about me? Good luck. Does the rabbit write about the hound? Does the chicken write about the fox?

He got up and came over to her. Write about this, he murmured, standing behind her, pulling her robe down over her shoulders, leaning down to lick the skin of her neck. So, he said, beside her ear, you were bored, were you? You won't be bored here. He slid the robe down her back and lifted her to her feet. Have you ever done it bent over the kitchen table? he asked. She slid out of his grasp, her cheeks flushed. Do you think, he asked her, that you will escape me? Yes, she cried excitedly. Impossible, he said softly, pronouncing it the French way. He reached out for her quickly, pinning her arms by her sides. Now my darling, he said, you have provoked me. Bend over, he said softly. No, she said. He pressed her down. She laughed. Holding her down with one hand, he slid the silk up over her bottom and spanked her lightly. She felt him up against her. He put his face for a moment into the curve of her backbone and kissed her. Now darling? he asked.

———————

Don't go down, I told them. He shook his head. A man in a uniform stands on a street with a bullhorn and they can't wait. He lifted the teapot and poured her a cup. In the middle of breakfast they jump up. Like puppets jerked on a string. Drink, he ordered her. He rubbed at his breastbone. What was the hurry? Later they stood like oxen in the central square for twelve hours. Crowded together. Lowing. He picked up a postcard lying on the table. Peered into the baroque architecture and gray sky and threw it down. That's the Jews for you, he said. Couldn't wait to die. What's the matter. Why don't you drink? he asked. Too dark for you? He lifted the cover of the teapot and peered in. It's as black as night in there, he remarked. Steeped too long. Drink it anyway darling. A little bitterness doesn't hurt. He poured himself some tea. The mother was thin with a long thin neck and short hair. She had the blinking eyes of a bird. A bird with blue eyes. When her eyes moved her head moved. Just like a bird. He drank from the cup and his dark eyes regarded her over the rim. She didn't look Jewish. She might have gotten out if she had had her wits about her. But not with them. The father and the child looked Jewish all right. Those fearful eyes. He tore off a piece of bread and chewed angrily. No mistaking them. The crumbs fell onto his collarbone. He wiped his mouth with his palm.

I used to go into the girl's room at night after the lights were out. She was thirteen but she looked younger. I would climb into her bed. Lying stiff as a board she would let me touch her above the waist. There was nothing there to speak of. But it passed the time. And it was warm in those girl-scented sheets. He frowned. Drink. Don't let it get cold. Do I have to do everything for you? Maybe I should feed you with an eyedropper. Like a little fledgling. Go on. Put in a few lumps of sugar. Didn't they teach you anything in that fancy home of yours? My grandfather, may he rest in peace, used to hold a lump between his teeth and drink his tea through it. Sweeten it on the way down. He leaned across the table and ran his hand down her cheek. Shall I teach you my angel? Hold it there for you between your pointed little teeth until you can do it on your own? He looked at her slyly with narrowed eyes. Or would you bite me you whore. He leaned back in his seat. Come and sit on my lap, he told her. Let me lick you. Let me bite you under the arm. Why do you shave under there. Women should grow a thicket of hair under their arms. To remind a man of the other thicket.

Oh darling, he moaned, come over here and sit on my lap. Let me feel you. She drank her tea. Come my baby. Come to me. He studied her appraisingly. You look like the women before the war. Full-bodied. Sly eyes. And that full lower lip. I'd like to put my tongue in there and lick it like an envelope. She smiled into her tea. He carved a piece of marbled sausage and put it in his mouth.

Don't go down I told them. Cozier to be shot at home. He licked the grease from his fingers. I tickled the girl under the arm in her little pink blouse. But this time she didn't laugh. Come on, I whispered. Stay behind. Think of all the fun we'll have. Her hair had been tightly braided and fastened with barrettes. Stay. Let them go without us. Her eyes widened and she clung weeping to her mother's arm. Stay. I even pleaded. But she didn't want to be left behind. Not on such an important outing. He drank his tea slowly. Neither did I for that matter, he said after a moment. He rolled a cigarette from the small pile of tobacco on the table. Gathered the copper strands into the white paper. But I wasn't going out into the street with a neat little suitcase and a jaunty hat to be packed into a train. He tapped his head. Too smart a Jew for that. When the voice came over the loudspeaker for the second time they didn't hesitate. The mother rinsed the cups and turned them upside down to dry before she left. A good hausfrau right up until the end. The smoke curled out from his nostrils. She dried her hands and put on her gloves but she couldn't get the fingers in right. Nerves. He tried to help her but he couldn't keep his hands still either. We didn't say goodbye. What for. The mother told me to look after things and lock up if I went out. Ha, he cried. The door closed behind them. And I crawled up into the attic the size of a rat's hole to lie down in the dust and wait. He was quiet for a moment drawing on his cigarette.

After a while when it grew silent outside I began to wish I had gone out in the street with the rest of them. Just when it grew silent as a tomb and I thought I might be the last one left on earth. He kept his cigarette between his lips. I called out to Him. After all He was the only one left. God, I said. No wonder you have so few friends these days. If this is the way you treat them. He shrugged. He didn't answer. He had already turned his face away. She waited in silence. The steam rose up from her tea and she placed both hands around the cup. You must have been terrified, she said quietly. His eyes darkened. What do you know? he shouted. Stay out of my story. He pulled a shred of tobacco from his tongue. What do you know, he muttered. What can you possibly know. How carefully they packed, he said with contempt. Shall we take this? Shall we be needing that? He laughed briefly. What a colossal joke. He looked at her steadily. You don't know, he said. It's another world. He sighed wearily. Never mind, never mind, he said after a minute. Let me make you laugh darling. Let me spin an egg on my head. Let me wear my trousers on my ears like a donkey. He reached over and pulled up a corner of her mouth. Smile, my sweetheart. Everything is all right. A man went into a synagogue. Rabbi, he said . . . No, better yet let's go to bed.

Come to bed darling, he said urgently, pulling her into the bedroom. Dig a hole in the woods, he said, pulling back the quilt, and I will crawl in. A rabbit hole for the rabbit to hide in, dark and still. He got into bed and held her tightly against him. Cover me with leaves, he whispered. No predators. What are you saying? she whispered. Don't talk like that. She stroked his dry hair. His eyes were wide open with alarm. Where shall I hide him? he asked her. Quick. What? she asked. Hide what? Open your legs darling. Let me hide him inside of you. No one will find him there, between your white thighs. Let him in darling with his missing piece. That's the safest place of all. She felt the beating of his heart against her. But the war's over, she panted, trying to enclose him, the war is over. My poor darling, he said sorrowfully, the war will never be over.

I will tell you something strange, said Joseph. One evening along the Herengracht, I thought I saw the girl. What girl? asked Kitty. Hetty, my foster sister who had been taken away. It was not a good idea to be wandering along there at night, even with papers. The fog lay over the canal and I could barely see my way in front of me. I had found a basement room where I stayed and I was on my way back there. And suddenly out of the fog appeared a young girl in a dark blue woolen coat with shiny gold buttons. Just like my Hetty's. She had the same dark hair pulled back with barrettes, the same eyes. Is it you? I asked her. What are you doing here? She didn't answer me. It was her all right. Come, I said, it's dangerous out here. I have a room. I reached out my hand for hers but she disappeared into the fog. I searched for her every-where. Why didn't she come back? I would have saved her. I would have hidden her. Kitty was silent. He looked at her unseeing. I would have, he said haltingly, would have kept her safe until the end of the war. Why did she run off like that?

After the war he lived in Paris, in Tel Aviv, in New York, the South of France, Vienna, London. He had been unable to stay put. Always restless, he traveled constantly, for a few days, a week at the most, with a small overnight bag and a bent Austrian passport from twenty years before. It didn't matter where he went as long as he could go somewhere. But he was not happy in Venice either, or Florence or Budapest or Athens. And the great excitement with which he had set off evaporated soon after he had checked into his hotel and gone out to have a coffee on the square. It's just the same, he would say sadly, looking around. Nothing new here. And often he would leave the next day or the day after, earlier than planned. Sometimes, if the circus was coming to town he would wait. He loved the circus and began to hum the tune of the calliope before he even entered the tent. He had run away to join the circus when he was nine. But a man had found him sitting on the bank of the Danube with his small rucksack beside him, eating chocolate out of a napkin, and taken him home. He loved all the acts, tapped his foot to the music, exclaimed and clapped. He laughed when the clowns spilled out of the tiny car, although he had seen it a hundred times. When he left the tent, the old hopelessness took hold of him.

Together they had gone to Prague and Budapest. But each time, after only a day or two, they had taken the next train out. In Prague they had eaten pastries and listened to gypsy violins. On the second day, in the Jewish Museum, they had seen old Jewish objects displayed in glass cases: religious articles, a shawl, a book, a pair of shoes. Joseph had moved away, his face tight. As though we were all dead and gone, he said bitterly, a vanished race that left behind a cup and a few saucers, now entombed behind glass. Come on, he said, gripping her arm, we're getting out, we're leaving on the next train.

All that madness, all that energy tucked into a small wooden coffin? How is it possible? Is there no law of physics that prevents it? As though one asked a tall man to live in a muskrat's hole. It happened all the time during the war, said Joseph. People squeezed into closets, under floorboards, disappeared into a hole in the forest floor. One man curled up in a stove. And stayed for years. As though they were no bigger than a muskrat or a mouse. The metamorphosis of a man into a four-footed animal, or an insect, or a load of kindling. More astounding, he remarked, than any circus act. And shaking his head he would line a thin paper with long strands of tobacco and roll it up tightly. But not me, my darling. I was out and about with more girl-friends than you could count on the fingers of both hands. I did not choose to live huddled in a box.

She has brought one of Joseph's books with her. *The Collected Plays.* That is what has weighed down her suitcase. Black as night, the critics called them. Dark as pitch. A trip to the underworld. Bleaker than anything we've read in decades. A postwar Kafka. A writer of brilliant imagination. World without light or redemption. Outrageously comical. At his kitchen table he used to pull out yellowed clippings from the fifties and sixties and read the reviews to her over and over until she could recite them by heart. She unzips her overnight bag and takes out the book. On the cover a man with shadowed eyes stands beside a tree without leaves. After a moment, she turns to the back flap. It gives her a shock to see the photo of him again. Thirty years ago. Long before she knew him. When his wavy hair was still dark, his face unlined, his eyes already full of bitterness. But it's him. She studies his face. What is the meaning of it all, she wonders wearily. She no longer knows the difference between past and present. And one day her train trip will be a memory and the frozen fields green.

Have I told you about Marijke? In Amsterdam? During the war? Yes, replied Kitty, a hundred times. Did I tell you how luscious she was, with her full lips, her bright blue eyes, her white-blond hair? You did, said Kitty. But she saved my life. I know, replied Kitty. She gave me the money for my false papers. And all because I was so handsome. She picked me up on the street. I thought you were Italian, she whispered to me later, with your dark hair and dark eyes. She slept with men for money. She wouldn't have done it in peacetime. Are you sure? asked Kitty sharply. During the occupation everyone had to do what he could. It was another world. She came from a village in the north of Holland. She had the big hips and sturdy legs of a farm girl. What a sweetheart she was. Are you jealous? No, she lied. Of course not. It was nearly fifty years ago. He watched her carefully. Yes you are, he said triumphantly.

I remember Marijke's bag. A large black imitation leather bag. And in that bag she carried everything: black market cigarettes and a small square of chocolate from a lover, an orange beret, a little flask of scent, a change of underwear, a piece of bread, and always loose coins. Marijke did not believe in change purses. So when she paid she dug down into that large black pouch and pulled it out coin by coin, laughing, fumbling, exclaiming over what a mess it was in there. Is this right? she would ask, holding out a handful of coins. And because of that smile of hers and those big tits, no shopkeeper was ever angry with her for wasting his time. How sweet, said Kitty. What a jealous woman you are, said Joseph. The most jealous woman I've ever met. I'm talking about fifty years ago. I'm not jealous, said Kitty, pulling at a long strand of hair. He laughed. Not much. I told Marijke, he went on, that my dream was to crawl into that big dark purse and spend the rest of the war there. That made her laugh. What a sweetheart, he said softly. Kitty sat quietly, pulling at her lip, watching him across the great divide of the table.

She took me upstairs. Even though she knew I couldn't pay. The woman at the desk didn't want to let her take me up. Hey, she called out, her orange hair piled on top of her head, who's that you're taking up with you? Uncured meat. Let him age a little longer. But Marijke said I was her cousin and the woman shrugged. Do what you like. But see that your cousin pays. It wasn't long before she figured out there was something missing. I swear by my mother that I will never tell, she whispered, her hand on her heart. How could I not love her, as I put my head between her large breasts and the scent of motherhood filled my nostrils.

In the sixties I was in Amsterdam for a writers' conference. Walking along, I thought I saw her standing in line for a film. It was her profile, the upturned nose, the full lips, her white-blond hair. She even carried a large black handbag and stood, as Marijke used to, with one shoe off and the foot resting against the other ankle. I felt dizzy. My heart was racing. I could hardly walk. But somehow I managed to run. Marijke! I called out. Marijke! And then, just as I came close, the woman turned around. . . .

We used to meet in a cafe down by the docks. I would get there early and wait for her. Soon I would look up and see her in her belted coat with her big black purse over her shoulder, laughing at me with her big teeth, her hair streaming out. She would sit down next to me and put her mouth next to my ear. Oh I had a terrible one, she would say. But I take one look at you and I forget them all. She slept with Germans too and I thought they should only know who they shared her with. Even a German uniform didn't impress her. It was me she loved. I worried constantly she would give me away. Not on purpose but after a few schnapps I thought she might get sentimental and mention her handsome boyfriend from Vienna. Kitty frowned. How could you stand it? Oh darling, he said, how naive you are. Did I have a choice? Did she? We wanted to stay alive.

Hour after hour he talked to her about Marijke and Amsterdam during the war, over and over again until finally she grew pale and irritable. I'm tired of the war, she said at last. Ho ho, he would cry, knocking his spoon against his cup. You're tired of the war? You? The spoon rang out. Born after it was all over? How tired do you think I am?

The old woman across the aisle is reading a small Bible, her chin quivering as she follows the lines with a reddened finger and then turns the thin page. She will call Henri as soon as she gets to Amsterdam. He always picks up on the first or second ring. Attentive, eager. Once in a while, perversely, she waits a moment or two before she speaks. Sometimes she thinks she has followed her parents' imperatives: safety, security. There is nothing better, her father would say, than to sit beneath the light of one's own lamp. Do you love me more than you loved him? Henri asks her. Darling, she says, kissing him, what a question.

Beyond the fields a row of trees has been planted. The delicate bare branches are lifted like lacework against the white sky. My mother, Joseph told her, came from a village in the Ukraine. They wore headscarves and cracked boots, and when she came to Vienna she felt ashamed. Still, she remembered her village, the lowing of cows, the yellow fields, the candlelight. She had blue eyes, my mother, and blond hair. My father was born in Vienna. He was a city boy, knew his way around electric lights, streetcars, bathtubs, bordellos. He told her to throw away the headscarves and come into the twentieth century. He forbade her to bring out the Sabbath candles or to mumble blessings over the flames.

But my mother came from a religious family and she couldn't forget entirely. She took me sometimes to a dim basement room in Vienna. There the candles flickered, the eastern melodies knocked against the small high windows while on the narrow wooden benches sat religious Jews. She would take my arm before we separated to opposite sides of the room. And leaning down she would whisper, This is our little secret. You mustn't tell your father. Yes, I would assure her, our secret. I sat with the men, Polish Jews in black with thick unruly eyebrows and small satin yarmulkes. Every time my eyes would catch hers she would frown and shake her head, pointing to the man who was reading Hebrew in a singsong monotone from a small ragged prayer book. On the way home she would buy me a little cake. But suddenly we stopped going. Why? asked Kitty. Why? Because one day I told him.

He flew into a rage of course. Shouted at her. Told her she was sinking back into her shtetl ways. He told her we were modern and enlightened, real Austrians, not remnants from the Middle Ages. My mother stood very still, her hand at her throat, her face flushed and said nothing. When he was

finished with his tirade, she went into the kitchen to pre-
pare dinner. But why? asked Kitty. Why did you tell him?
The smoke seeped out from his nose and mouth. Because,
he began. He shrugged. Because I loved her.

We were not really Jews, you know. We didn't go to syn-
agogue. We didn't speak Yiddish. We weren't real Jews.
Then who was? asked Kitty. The Ostjuden, he said with
disdain. The Yiddish Jews in the caftans. Those were the
Jews. Not us. My father wore a stiff collar and a dark suit.
He spoke good German and his clients were mostly non-
Jews. I sang patriotic songs at school and saluted the flag.
And when I left, he said quietly, I left because I wanted to.
Nobody kicked me out.

My mother looked more Austrian than the Austrians. She
wanted to be a playwright. She worshipped the Yiddish
playwrights and wrote sentimental plays in small lined
notebooks. One, I remember, took place in a Polish village. A very romantic story of a young girl who wants to
marry the man she loves. But her father forbids her because the man is leaving to seek his fortune in Warsaw and
he doesn't want his daughter to abandon religious ways.

Does the girl run away to be with him? asked Kitty. No, he replied. She marries the man of her father's choice whom she does not love. She read this play to me several times. I thought the girl cried too much but I liked it. I was only ten. Also I thought she should have gone to Warsaw with the man she loved. I told my mother to change the ending but she said that was the whole point, people sometimes had to do things out of duty or obedience that they didn't want to do or that they regretted the rest of their lives. Somehow my father got hold of that notebook. He sat at the table reading bits of it aloud and rocking with laughter. Every time the girl wept he laughed his head off. I'm sorry, he said to her, his eyes wet with tears. But the way you describe her unhappiness . . . and he would start in again. At last my mother put down her napkin and left the table. She's too sensitive, he said to me and winked. Like all women.

My mother deserved better than she got. From him too. At the opening party for *Sticks and Stones*, Dalya, love of my life, offered a toast to my mother. To the first playwright in the family, she said. I hated her for that, the bitch. Weakening me when I had to be strong.

———

He cut the dark bread against his chest, drawing the knife toward him. It's a little old but it won't hurt us. The dark crust was cracked and he cradled the loaf against his chest. I can't throw bread away, he told her. Not an end, not a morsel, not a crumb. Can you understand that? Do you know what a loaf of bread was trading for in those days? The blade traveled with difficulty through the hard bread. A diamond wedding ring, a silver candelabra, a stack of bills. And sometimes, as the Bible says in another context, its price was beyond rubies. By the way, he added, the one who received the bread figured he had made an excellent trade. He put down the loaf and handed her a slice. Go on, he said, take it. Now it's free. He slathered his slice with goose fat. How happy we would have been with this. Happy? We would have been ecstatic. He opened the drawer and brought out two petrified ends of bread. He winked. Just in case, he told her and put them back in the drawer. You never know. Better to be prepared. He wiped the grease from his mouth. People kept a crust of bread for months. Picked at it crumb by crumb. Savored it like it was pâté de foie gras. If you don't know, he said, his mouth full, how sweet the taste of bread is, a day old, even three, you know nothing about life.

I want to know, said Kitty urgently. Joseph looked at her carefully. Do you? he asked. And maybe you think I will teach you? I can't teach you, he said. For the simple reason that I don't know. Still. After everything. But you must, said Kitty urgently. He laughed briefly. And what if I don't? Do you really believe that God brought order out of chaos as it tells us in Genesis? Can one live a day on this earth and continue to believe that? But there has to be some kind of order, insisted Kitty leaning forward. He shook his head. It's all chaos. Madness. A funfair of distortions. You don't know where you are. Not for a moment. We live in madness. And if you cry out to God for some explanation, what does He answer? He doesn't. Like some Greek god he has gone away to the ends of the earth to visit his brother the Wind or his sister the Breeze. And while He is gone, they encircle the weak, drive them into crumbling concrete pastures and massacre them. It can't be, cried Kitty. You're too sentimental, he told her. You wouldn't have lasted long back then. He poured out two small glasses of schnapps and the liquid spilled over the rims. He paid no attention. Forget everything you learned at your mother's knee. He shook his head with disgust. So sentimental, the Jews. So softhearted with their big brown eyes. He fixed her with a bitter stare. Be ready for any madness. Be ready to hate. And most important, travel alone. Maybe then you'll have a chance to survive. Kitty began to cry silently, her eyes blurred with tears. It can't be so bleak, she pleaded with him. Please Joseph, not that bleak. He shrugged and pulled his white handkerchief from the pocket of his robe. Take this, darling. She reached for the handkerchief and pressed it to her eyes. He watched her impassively. Go ahead, he said, cry. I would cry too if I could.

He led her into the bedroom but for once their lovemaking was dry. They pulled at each other angrily but could not join. He thrust and thrust and she pushed against his chest with both hands in her frustration. There was no pleasure but only a relentless sterile heat. It doesn't matter, said Joseph at last, exhausted. We're alive. They clung together, breathing heavily. He ran a humid hand through her hair. Try to sleep, he said. What else can we do?

I was born on the coldest night of the century, he said. The Danube froze over. And my mother, he continued,

brought forth her first and only son. At once I grew a
head of thick black hair and when I was only two the
maid, a young girl from the country, used to sleeping with
the cows, let me crawl on top of her and sleep there, between her warm breasts. . . . Kitty shook her head. He
laughed and pinched her cheek. Mitzi. My first love. She
talked baby talk to me even when I was eight. She bathed
me. She dressed me. Sometimes I persuaded her to feed
me with her own fingers. Le petit roi, said Kitty. Mitzi
wore her blond hair braided and twisted into tight circles
over her ears. I touched them sometimes and they were as
hard as hemp. She was always babbling about ghosts and
spirits and sprites who lived in the chimneys and demons
who entered into cows and drove them mad. Sometimes
she carried me halfway across town to a Catholic church.
It was empty in the afternoon and she would go down on
her knees in front of the Virgin Mary and I would sit in a
pew and bang my heels against the wood until she got up
and crossed herself and led me out. Why is he hanging
there? I asked her. Her father beat her at home and she
slept in the same bed with her father and brothers. Her
mother had died when she was a baby. Poor girl. Think of
what went on in that big wooden carved bed in the dead
of winter. What I required of her wasn't much in compar-
ison. Sometimes she would fall asleep before I did. I didn't

like that. When I heard the slow whistle of her breath I would pinch her awake again.

After the Anschluss she could no longer work for us. No female Aryan servants under the age of forty-five could work in Jewish households. She wept and packed up her few things. We didn't have much but my mother gave her an old coat of hers with a rabbit collar. She kissed my mother's hand and a torrent of Austrian dialect poured out of her which I couldn't understand. She cried and wiped her nose on a flowered handkerchief. Then she turned to me, her eyes red. She put down her things and held out her arms to me. But I wouldn't say goodbye to her. She pleaded with me to give her a kiss but I couldn't. I even turned my back on her. My mother reprimanded me, reminded me of how much Mitzi loved me. But I refused to turn around. Mitzi left and a minute later I changed my mind and raced out after her. But it was too late. She had disappeared. I didn't know that in a few months I too would be leaving with a little case. But Mitzi was going home and I . . .

One night late, Joseph decided to teach her to play poker. At the end of the war, he said, dealing out the cards, I began to walk. It seemed that everyone in Europe was walking somewhere. Through rubble, through bombed-out towns and villages. Everywhere the landscape was filled with people on the move. Not just the roads. The fields and the forests too. I slept at the side of the road. Like Jacob I had a rocky pillow, but no holy ladder reaching to heaven appeared against the night sky. I was not the only one to sleep under the stars. Sometimes I awoke in darkness to find the shivering forms of those who had come back from the dead nearby, groaning in their sleep. They lay down like shorn sheep on the same hillside. I could not be near them. They cried out, their limbs twitched. In those days I had only one idea and that was to get to Marseille and onto the next boat sailing for Haifa. I did not dare to go back to Vienna. Not yet. My plan was to get to Paris. From there to Marseille, where you could get on a ship for Haifa. I began to walk. I walked for weeks. In Rotterdam I got lucky. There was a train leaving for Paris. We squeezed in until we could hardly breathe. A donkey would have been faster.

Now wait, he said, don't look yet. Let me explain first. Only three cards? she asked in surprise. At the end of the war, he said, the train took three weeks to get to Paris. In that packed train we played cards from morning till night. We played with the greatest enthusiasm. Imagine. People young and old. Most of them weighing no more than a child. Playing cards all day and night as though they were still children. No jobs, no homes, no bills, no families. Meanwhile as the cards were dealt out, as the train neared some kind of destination, we tried not to think what in God's name we were going to do with these lives of ours. Lives we had managed to save against all odds.

Suddenly he began to shuffle the cards at lightning speed. They flew up his arm as though blown by the wind and tumbled back down into his hand. He lifted his hand and the cards rose up in the air like a flock of birds and then fell back in a neat rectangle in his palm. My God, said Kitty awestruck. Where did you learn that? He smiled happily, his cheeks flushed. He shuffled quickly and the deck fanned out in his palm. He pressed lightly on the cards. Come my sweethearts, he chanted, come my little birds, and the four aces flew out of the deck. How is it possible, cried Kitty. You are not the only one, he said proudly, other people were frightened too.

———

On that train to Paris, he said, there was a group of children who came through the crowded cars performing. They sang, recited childish verses, led by a man who had once sung on the stage in Vilna and Warsaw. Even Vienna. He was a tall man, emaciated now, with long limbs and sunken cheeks. Now it happened that one night as the train rolled through the darkness they came through the car I was in. The children sang their snatches of songs, recited their little poems. Then unaccountably the man began to sing an old Yiddish song. Everyone screamed at him to stop. Take your old sentimental songs somewhere else, we don't want to hear them. Get out, they cried, and take your schmaltz with you. They were in a rage. Poor man. He left the car in tears and they jeered at him as he went. Why? asked Kitty. It's so unjust. He dealt the cards. Now, he said. Look at your cards. What do you have? But Kitty was looking at him still. I don't understand. You don't? Not one of those Jews wanted to open his heart even a crack to the other life, the life before. His only hope was to keep it sealed up tight. Now, he said wearily, look at your cards and tell me what you have.

———

We boarded the ship in the port of Marseille. A rotten crate that stank of mildew and oil. Hundreds of us pressing up the gangplank while all around the blinding sun glinted off the sea. A shipful of exhausted Jews racing to claim a few feet of deck. He fished out a herring from the jar and the brine dripped from his fingers. Have one, he offered, holding it out to her. Kitty shook her head. You have never, he said to her, known such heat. We lay on deck, shirtless. Below it was even worse. We rigged up shelters with sheets, with shirts, with nightgowns. Anything we could find to put between us and the rays of the sun. Babies cried. The men played cards. The women pulled their skirts up over their knees. What did it matter? All modesty was forgotten. We were frying. And the closer we came to Palestine the more relentless the heat. In two thousand years we had forgotten what the southern sun can be. No one moved. We lay listlessly and waited for evening. As soon as the sun set I went below with Zenia, a young Hungarian girl from Szeged. She began to tell me her story, a litany of disaster. But I had already heard so many of those stories, I was stuffed full of those stories. Did I need to hear more? I stopped her and told her to undress. But I will tell you the truth. When she pulled off her dress and I saw her ribs pressing out through the skin of her chest, her hipbones without any flesh, God forgive me I couldn't do it. I told her I was not well. I told her I had stomach troubles and I helped her back on with her tattered dress. She gazed at me with her motionless black eyes. What could I do? I had had enough of the ossuaries of Europe.

He cut a thick slice of rye and slathered it with butter. We came into the harbor of Haifa at night, a clear tropical night, and saw the outlines of palms against the starry sky. We were all up on deck, avid for a view of the Promised Land. Every moonlit building seemed blessed to us, every stray dog a prophet. The gangplank was laid down and we came into the Holy Land. Some people knelt and kissed the ground. Not me. I had other things on my mind. Why don't you eat? he asked indicating the bread. I don't want you getting too thin. The harbor, lit with searchlights, was swarming with Jews. They ate pistachios out of little paper bags, watching everyone who came down the gangplank, hoping to find an uncle, a sister, a mother or father who hadn't been heard from since 1939.

———

In the morning before the sun rose trucks came to take us to the transit camp. I saw the Carmel, those mountains thick with pines, and the bright blue sky whose canopy had arched over Abraham, Isaac and Jacob. My parents were Zionists. How happy they would have been to see me there, where Jacob dreamed and Isaac found a bride and Abraham bound his son, there in the midst of sand, clinging windblown scrub and the bleating of Arab sheep. In the camp we lived in tents, behind barbed wire, but at least this time the dusty soil beneath our feet was holy ground.

He scratched at his chest. An uncle came to see me when I was in the transit camp. He had been Leon. Now his name was Arye. I had never laid eyes on the man. A brother of my father's who had left for Palestine when he was barely sixteen. He peered at me through the barbed wire. He could not come in. I could not go out. So, he said to me, here you are. He pulled out a white handkerchief and blew his nose with a flourish. Like my father used to do it. You have your aunt's chin, he told me. And your grandfather's nose. His gaze wandered. He looked pale in the brilliant

sunlight, as though he had wandered into the wrong cli-
mate. He told me he had a hat factory outside of Tel Aviv.
They made whatever was needed, military caps, yarmulkes,
black fedoras. He promised to send me a khaki cap. Unless,
God forbid, you want a yarmulke. So, so. You made it out
of Europe. You should have brought your parents. He studied my face. Where were you? Amsterdam, I replied. You
went in the wrong direction, he informed me.

He had a curious manner of rubbing his hands like a fly
rubs his legs together. He was doing it now. Terrible, he
burst out suddenly. I told them to come. I told your father
even before 'thirty-eight. Sigmund, I said, get out. Get on a
boat and come to Palestine. The man spoke German with a
strange intonation after all these years. Why didn't they
come? I was ready to put them up until they found a place
of their own. I told him there was a place for him at the factory. What madness. He squinted up at the sky. The ham-
sin is coming, he remarked. The wind. The sky turns red as
though it were the end of days. It's not. Just chemicals in
the air. His dry white hair stood up from his narrow forehead. Well take care of yourself, he said at last and gave me
a kind of salute. His trousers were dusty, his blue shirt was
missing a button. Then he turned back and fumbling in his

pocket, he drew out a few shekels. I reached my fingers through the barbed wire and took the coins. I'll be out soon, I told him, and on my way to a kibbutz. He looked at me angrily. Why didn't they come when they still had the chance? I offered to send money. I even offered to put them up. I pleaded with them. What were they thinking? He was shouting by now. I turned the coins over in my palm. Your father was always like that. Stubborn as a donkey. Didn't listen to anyone. His face was mottled with anger. Sigmund, he cried out.

Joseph went to the refrigerator and sniffed at a plate of cheese. Stink cheese I call it, he said. It's Limburger. Kitty wrinkled her nose. Try it darling, don't be so proper. Some of the most delicious things in life smell bad. He brought over the plate and cut her a thin slice of bread. Limburger Käse. What could be better? Eat it. Don't hold it in front of you as though it were a dead bird. It's a delicacy. He shook his head. Must I teach you everything? Did you learn nothing at all in that upright household of yours?

As soon as I escaped from behind barbed wire I went looking for the remnants. I rose early in the morning and traveled by bus to the office where they kept the lists. Lists with the names of thousands of Jews, arranged alphabetically. Even so the heat burned into the metal roof of the bus and turned it into an oven. Even the chickens grew limp. I was dizzy by the time I arrived. The place was swarming with people. Behind a makeshift desk sat the secretary, a plump girl with bright red curls. The chatter of a hundred languages came to my ears. I felt faint and squeezed onto a long bench. There were shouts and cries but they seemed far away. At last my head cleared. I got up and pushed my way through the crowd to the lists. You have never seen so many names. I found the L's. But I wasn't ready to look. Not yet. I saw the secretary smiling at me, her eyelids lowered suggestively. On her desk a small green plant was dying out. There were Lanzbergs. But no Lanzbergs I knew. Only me with the name of my kibbutz beside it. Then I understood. It was a clerical error. My parents had been left off the list by mistake. In a day or two I would come back and look again. And there I would see Lanzberg, Sigmund. Lanzberg, Miriam. Lanzberg? asked Kitty in surprise. Why Lanzberg? Because that was our name. Kitty stared at him. Joseph Kruger is not your real name? He slathered on the Limburger until it looked like mortar. I have had many names, he said with a shrug. The fate of a Jew my darling. He must constantly metamorphose to stay one step ahead, to remain alive. But what name were you born with? Let me see, he said. Now what was it? Stop it, cried Kitty. As I remember it was Friedrich Lanzberg. She looked at him dumbfounded. Friedrich Lanzberg? Who is that? It's somebody else. Yes, agreed Joseph. Kitty pressed her fingers to her forehead. Why didn't you tell me? Is it so important? he asked lazily. We all had to change our names. It was our only chance. But the war is over, said Kitty, you can change it back now. He looked at her pityingly. How little you understand. We couldn't wait to shed those Jewish names we had tried so desperately to change or conceal when it was a matter of life and death. We wanted to begin again. A new name, a new self, a new life. We wanted to forget. Did it work? He looked at her. What do you think? You should have told me, insisted Kitty. He shrugged. I'm telling you now. She shook her head. I feel I don't know who you are. He gave a short laugh. Do you think I know?

In my passport I am still Friedrich Lanzberg. At reception desks of hotels everywhere they still call me Mr. Lanzberg. I would like to tell them that Friedrich Lanzberg disappeared in 1940 and that a Dutchman by the name of Jan

Vinke took his place. But at hotel reception desks everywhere they are busy and have no time for old stories. Except once in a long while. Late one night I checked into a hotel in Frankfurt. There behind the desk stood a stooped man in a faded maroon uniform that had seen better days. His thin black hair was slicked down over his head, his eyes were rimmed in shadows. He looked twenty years older than me. This man and I looked at each other and I thought: there is something familiar here. But I could not put my finger on it. And then he said to me in Viennese, Is that Fritz Lanzberg? My eyes searched his face. Rudy Hirschfeld, he whispered. Now Robert Hartley. We had been at school together. Well well, I said to him, we're still alive. He came out from behind the desk (it was so late everyone had gone to bed). He brought out a bottle of cognac and we exchanged stories through the night. So, said Rudy finishing off the cognac, you made it to the Promised Land. And was it as promised?

Imagine that, Joseph said, lining up two small glasses, I was in the Garden of Eden and I could not wait to get out. Kitty reached for her glass and drank it down carefully. I did not need an apple or a snake to convince me. Or an

Eve, added Kitty. Certainly not an Eve, he agreed. Although there was one of course. More than one.

Oh my darling, how you would have loved me then. I was so handsome, with my dark curls. In the kibbutz I had as many girls as there are grains of sand in the Negev. They reached up their bare arms to pull down oranges beneath a Jewish sky. Could there be anything more delicious? I had them to my tent one after another. But the kibbutz leader expected me to pull my weight. I was told to roll up my sleeves and get to work. As you know my sweetheart, I am not cut out for this sort of thing. I had soon had enough of collective life. Stay, they said to me, my fellow Jews, as they picked oranges in the orchards of the Lord. Why go back to Europe where the darkness will not be dispelled for a hundred years? I couldn't stay. I tried. The heat drove me insane. And who needs fresh oranges three times a day. Besides, there were too many Jews. I began to long for the gray skies of Europe.

I remember Eva, a delicious girl from the Ukraine with a tilted nose and blond hair like flax. She wore her shorts rolled up and a checked blouse. I used to watch her in the fields when she bent over and then I forgot to pick oranges, I forgot everything. It took me not one day but two to lure her back to my tent. She cried out in Ukrainian but I understood her every word. He drank down a schnapps and wiped his mouth happily. But then calamity struck. Locusts? Boils? Plague? Much worse. Malka. My Hungarian misfortune. My first wife.

At night she took off the headscarf she wore all day and I lay down in the waves of her soft dark hair. We couldn't stop. We were insatiable. All night beneath the stars. Again and again. Until one day she became pregnant. She went around in a daze, ecstatic as a good Jewish wife who sways before the Sabbath candles. My child will be born in Eretz Israel, she kept repeating. As though she were carrying the Messiah. Get rid of it, I told her. I might as well have told her to throw herself under a train. She called me a brute, a monster, even a Nazi. What didn't she call me. He put down his cup. Did I want a screaming baby? Does a Jew want pogroms?

My father was a Zionist but he would have hated the Holy Land. This was a man who wore a suit no matter how hot the weather. Where are the boulevards, he would have asked, the coffeehouses, the chocolate shops, the restaurants with their red velvet banquettes. Where does one find a music hall, an operetta. What kind of a civilization is this? He would have looked around at all the sand in despair, he would have mocked the tuneless patriotic songs. And he would have searched in vain for the women with bright hair and brighter lips, in stockings and corsets and dainty high-heeled shoes. Work in a hat factory? God forbid.

One day an old mistress of his looked me up. My name was Yossi by then. But I was still listed as Lanzberg. She came to see me in the kibbutz, a blowsy redhead in a silk print dress left over from her Vienna days. Inge, her name was. She wanted to talk about my father and I let her talk. She had been in love with him. I could see the top of her breasts artfully arranged above the tight silk, but they were no longer smooth or firm. She remembered his songs, his jokes, the name of his cologne. You don't look much like him, she said, studying me. Well maybe the nose. She did not ask about my mother. Her neck was lined, her hands freckled. I was tired of all this talk of my father from her. But I did not know how to stop her. Even her Viennese got on my nerves. There was only one thing to do. Take her to bed. You took everyone to bed, remarked Kitty. He shrugged. Isn't that what women want?

Joseph, said Kitty looking down at her plate, I am like one of those grains of sand. No, my sweetheart, he said soothingly, you mustn't think like that. No one can compare with you. Liar, she said. No one at all. He came over and stood before her. Come to bed my darling, he said softly, pressing his hand into the opening of her kimono. I'll mount you as a stallion mounts his favorite mare. Let me forget in that cave of warm flesh. You'll cry out and move your soft white thighs. I'll bury myself so deep they'll never get me out. That's the only place he's safe, he murmured, when he's hiding inside that warm hole.

My darling I was twenty-eight when you were born. I had already lived through the war, been married, had a child. When you were having your diapers changed, I was married to Malka and Anton was crawling all over the place, his little cheeks smeared with jam. He cried all the time. Why I don't know. What could I do? I was a baby myself. The heat in Palestine was unbearable. We lived above a candy store. And already Malka was unhappy with me. You monster, she would shout in her Hungarian accent, monster who has ruined my life and the life of my child. I will drown myself in the bathtub. One more thing and I will sink under the water and never come up. He snorted. That would be the day. The woman was as tough as nails. She didn't drown herself. Not Malka. But one day she packed up and left. And when I came home there was a note on the kitchen table. Don't try to find us, she wrote. What a hot night it was. I remember it still. The locusts shrilling. Not a breath of air. But many years later it was they who tried to find me. When Malka found out I was a famous writer, she suddenly became interested again. Did you see her? I saw her. Why not? I spent one night with her and the witch became pregnant. But this time she got rid of it. Kitty closed her eyes. So brutal, she murmured. Joseph pulled her down beside him. Brutal, he said to her. You don't know what brutal is. I'm so tired, said Kitty. Exhausted. How tired do you think I am, he asked her. Don't you ever think of anyone else, she asked, ever? She looked down at his nakedness. So many women had seen him naked. He did not belong to her at all. She turned her face away. He took her chin in his fingers and guided her back. He pressed his mouth up against her ear. I can't, he whispered. Imagine if I cared . . . And then she went away.

Twenty years later the bell rang. I opened the door and saw myself as I had been at that age. The same eyes, the same black curls, same nose. Anton had come to pay a visit to his long-lost father. Only he was sober and serious. Nothing like me. He measured out his life in coffee spoons as the poet says. I dug in with a shovel. There he was. My first-born. And all he could say to me in his sober and serious voice was why did you abandon us. It sounded biblical. I had to remind him that it was his mother who had taken him and left. But this was not the version he had heard. Joseph shrugged. Never mind. Everyone has his own version. He was a nice boy. He wanted to be an engineer. If he weren't my son I might even have liked him. Maybe he imagined I would suddenly clasp him in my arms or deliver a speech of apology or make a declaration of paternal love.

So what ever happened to your mother? I asked him at last. She had remarried it seemed soon after we separated. A Polish Jew who had crawled out of Bergen-Belsen more dead than alive (although he did not put it this way) and together the happy couple had conceived three more children—girls. As I said, he was a nice boy, but I couldn't be a father to him. Too much time had passed. I showed him a photo of myself when I was his age and he stared at it for a long time. He too saw how we resembled each other physically. Do you have a girlfriend? I asked him. He nodded. Her name is Dafna. She is studying to be a biologist. Well invite me to the wedding, I told him. About a year later he did. But I didn't go. Fly all the way to Tel Aviv? What for? He shook his head. Maybe I should have gone after all. He was my firstborn. What a sad story, said Kitty. Sad? replied Joseph. That's not sad. You don't know what sad is. Have a cookie, my angel. He pushed the plate toward her. Have two or three. You'll never be too zaftig for me.

He took a large white handkerchief from the pocket of his robe and sneezed loudly, drawing out the last part with a near shout. So needlessly theatrical, said Kitty, unimpressed. Shall I tell you a story about my sneeze? No, replied Kitty. Two middle-aged spinster sisters, both with long gray hair, live directly beneath me. One day I stepped into the elevator. One of the sisters was in there, her long gray hair pulled back with a pink ribbon. Oh Mr. Kruger, she said to me in her girlish voice. Last night when you sneezed, my sister fell out of bed. Kitty laughed. Well well, he said, so I can still cheer you up. And he replaced his handkerchief in the cavernous pocket of his robe.

A car on a small country road is racing the train, speeding through the deserted ribbon of road, the only thing that moves in the white motionless landscape. With which of his many names will he be buried? Which name will they carve into the cool white stone? A man with four names is by definition a madman, a schizophrenic who is split not in two but in four, he told her. Which of these selves is the real one? Are any of them? Are all of them? What are you doing with a madman? he wanted to know. Have you asked yourself this question? Never mind, he said to her, I'm not really here. Not even, asked Kitty, when you sleep with me? He smiled at her. Come here my beautiful girl. When I sleep with you I enter another country altogether. He held out his hand to her. Come my angel.

My son Anton remained in the Land of Israel, he remarked. He became a soldier in the Israeli Army. He sent me a photo of himself, tanned and strong, and I recognized my chin, my dark eyes, my wavy hair. I regretted that I had not gone to his wedding but when you do not grow up with a child . . . He was studying engineering. This means nothing to me. What is it? Building bridges? Laying pipes? No idea. In any case, this was the path he had chosen. He would have been about your age. Would have been? echoed Kitty. He is no longer alive, he said briskly. Now, let's talk of happier things. But Joseph, said Kitty, what happened? His mother that maniac gave birth to him in the kibbutz dispensary. Thirteen hours of labor. I thought the screams would never end. But she finally managed and he emerged red-faced and indignant. I was there. I took him up in my arms and was soon covered in more blood than a butcher. His eyes could not yet focus of course, but I felt somehow that we understood each other.

Malka went off with him when he was barely a year. As you know I did not see him again until he was twenty. Soon after I left the Promised Land. I had decided to go back to Europe. It seems I had not yet had enough. It was still dark when I left the kibbutz. As I walked toward the road with my small suitcase the sun came up, a burning red sun that lit up the orchards and the fields, the wells, the flat roofs of the kibbutz. I heard the voices of my Zionist parents. What madness is this? Leave the Promised Land? What kind of a Jew thinks like this? But I kept on, and when I heard the roar of the bus I put out my hand. As I boarded the bus in the warmth of the early morning sunlight, I thought of the grim and darkened skies of Europe. And of that spot on the banks of the Danube where I had rested with my school satchel, eating chocolate out of a napkin.

Later, when I was back in the ruins of Europe, I sometimes heard the voices of my parents as the moon hid behind the dark-edged clouds and the wind whistled through the chimney. And I felt I had betrayed them and all their dreams. What kind of a Jew . . . ? they seemed to say. I had no answer for them.

What happened to Anton? asked Kitty after a moment. He shrugged. Anton is no more. His mother wrote to me at the time. Only the Hungarians can weep like this. A tear-stained letter with all the details. He was out on patrol one night on the Lebanese border. A man in an Israeli uniform came up to him in the dark. Anton lowered his gun. It was a moonless night. And the man who was no Israeli pressed a weapon to his chest and fired. Where he had stolen the uniform from no one knew. Joseph took up his lighter in the shape of a rocket. He was twenty-four. I did not attend the funeral. I could not get there in time. He rolled a cigarette, licked the end and flicked the lighter. My parents have gone, my wives have disappeared, my sons are no longer here. It seems I am the only one left. And me? Kitty could not help asking. He appeared not to have heard, and gazing past her he drew in on his cigarette and pressed out small smoke rings one after the other.

The sky seems heavier, leaden the farther north they go. The villages and farms are run-down, fallen into disrepair. Rusted farm equipment lies here and there, its metallic wings and jaws softened by the dusting of snow. Kitty pulls her coat around her. Suddenly she wants to turn back. Why travel all this way and not see him, touch him, hear the sound of his voice? Are you looking for the coffeepot? he asked her one afternoon. Then follow me. He marched to the hall closet as though he were leading a brass band. Kitty laughed and followed close behind him. He remained for a moment before the door and then continued on to the closet in the living room. There he hesitated for a moment, marching in place, and in an abrupt about-face led her back to the kitchen cabinet where the pot was kept. There's your coffeepot, he said. Kitty laughed. You find me irresistible, he remarked. No, protested Kitty. Liar, he said. Do you think I don't know women?

Henri did not understand why she was going. What for? Such a long trip. And in the freezing cold. Sometimes she watches Henri at his drafting table with his rulers and his pens. He works so intently, so silently, and draws such straight lines, his head with its brush of stiff hair bent over the plans. A solid man. Reliable. Unchanging. You don't still love him, do you? he asked suddenly this morning in bed, his shoulder pressing insistently against hers.

I had a friend in the kibbutz, Joseph told her once. His name was Amnon. When his father died, Amnon hitched a ride on the back of a truck to be in time for the funeral, holding carefully over his arm his father's best suit, his white shirt, his tie. When he arrived breathless at the embalmer's, the man took the clothes in order to dress the corpse. And the shoes? asked the undertaker. But Amnon had forgotten them. Because of what he had done (and there was no time to make the trip back to the kibbutz), his father would not have shoes to walk in when he got to the next world. This haunted his dreams. He could not forgive himself. He pictured his father barefoot in his coffin. You should have painted a pair and placed them over his feet, Joseph told him, just as the Egyptians painted eyes so that the deceased could see in the other world.

She hopes that Joseph has his shoes. And that they have dressed him in one of his innumerable blue shirts. He seemed to have an endless supply of them. Aside from his bathrobe she never saw him in anything else. Where did you get so many blue shirts? Kitty asked him once. I have thirty of them, he told her. My girlfriends gave them to me. You have thirty girlfriends? One of them, he replied, gave me twenty-nine. And smiling, he pinched her cheek. She would watch him reach into the shelf and take one out, tearing the shirt off the cardboard, unbuttoning the two top buttons and pulling it on over his head. No other man puts on a shirt like that, she told him. He unbuttons the whole thing first. Good, he said to her tucking the shirttails into his pants, then this makes a change. And he would take a small brush to his wild hair.

One night he turned on the radio that stood dusty and out of date on a shelf. He turned the dial until he found a station that played old 1940s dance tunes. Listen to that, he said in wonder. I remember a song called "Stardust." It came from faraway America. Where everyone wanted to go. Longed to go. America was life and freedom. And we had heard that the streets were paved with gold. It seemed that in America they were always dancing. While over in Europe we were dying out. Kitty saw a quick movement behind him, along the rim of the kitchen counter. It's a mouse, she announced. The tiny creature ran along the silver rim. He went over and banged his hand loudly on the counter and the mouse stopped, paralyzed. But in a moment it began to run again and disappeared. What shall we call her? asked Kitty. Martina, he said. If she came once, she'll come again. Particularly with the sea of bread crumbs to be found on that counter, added Kitty. Well clean it up then, said Joseph, like a good wife. One of these days, she said lightly, I'm going to murder you. Oh darling, he replied, you can't murder me. I'm already dead. Don't say that, cried Kitty. He smiled. No, he agreed getting up. He grabbed her arm. Come, he urged her, pulling her close, let's dance. Put your head against my chest. Lean against me. That's how they did it in the photos in *Life* magazine which the American soldiers brought. At the end of the war we were too tired to dance, he said as he led her back and forth. We wanted to lie down and sleep for a hundred years. But after a while we began to move our feet and all the fun began. Years and years of fun. We were celebrating the end of the war for years. In a daze. In a dream. He held her tightly and closed his eyes for a moment. It fits, he said quietly. What a miracle. And his hands tightened around her waist.

But after a moment his grip tightened. You whore, he whispered. If you knew how you excite me. He led her to the table, bending her over, pressing her against it until she cried out. That's it, he told her, cry out. Go ahead. Cry out until someone hears you at last. Then he turned her around and kissed her mouth tenderly. I didn't mean it, my angel, he murmured. Then why do you say it? she asked pulling away from him. Because I love you, he replied. You make it so difficult, said Kitty wearily. I have to. Always? Always. He ran his finger along her bottom lip. No, she said shaking him off, you won't pull me back in. Let me feed you dates and honey cakes, he said softly. Why shouldn't we press open the immense and creaky iron doors of Paradise and enter together. Kitty shook her head. I don't feel like forgiving you. He held her tightly, his forehead pressed against hers. Don't give up on me, he pleaded. Not yet.

He had nightmares, dreamed that he was running, choking, drowning. He dreamed that the lights went out, the sky fell down, the sun was blotted out. In the old days he could not sleep without a woman beside him. Any woman. To wake him as soon as he began to shout. I would like, he said, to raise a monument to all women. They have saved me at every twist and turn. How many of them, in the years after the war, were awakened by my screaming in the middle of the night. How they put up with it I'll never know. In those days my nightmares began as soon as I laid my head on the pillow. Sometimes, when I lay with one of my hundreds of women, I imagined that my grandfather with his dark eyes, his beard as soft as grass, stood at the end of the bed shaking his head, muttering, Shame shame. When a wicked man dies, according to medieval Jewish law, he is buried with a stone on his shroud, the stoning that he merited in life but which has not been carried out. Is that you? she asked him. Oh my darling, he replied, one stone is not enough for me. They should weigh down my shroud with boulders.

But you, my sweetheart, said Joseph, squeezing her against him, kissing her mouth. You are still a child. You don't know what death is. You won't die for another hundred years. I'm thirty-two, protested Kitty. A child, he repeated, smoothing down her hair. No, my angel, he said, pinching her cheek. For me you will always be a young girl. And with him, she remained a young girl. It was when she left him, left him and went out into the air, that she began to age.

I never told my children anything. I'm telling you more than I ever told them. They were afraid of me. Anton, the first one, Malka's son, as you know I didn't see until he was grown. And Stefan. Stefan? asked Kitty in surprise. My son with Lena, my second wife. He shrugged. Stefan didn't dare. How I fathered a child like that I don't know.

———————

When Stefan was little, he used to cling all the time. Wrap his arms piteously around your leg, cling to his mother's ankle or neck, whatever happened to be in reach. This used to drive me insane. Act like a man, my boy, I would say to him but he would only reach out his arms with that tremulous yearning in his eyes. He was thin with sticklike legs and wide pleading eyes. Dear God in heaven, I said to my wife, he looks like a Jew already. That's all I need. We had better feed him red meat and teach him to salute. Why shouldn't he be strong and independent, powerful. From where did he get this cringing look? If I didn't know better I would say he grew up in the ghetto.

But that madwoman Lena was in another world. She didn't hear a word I said. She was sewing curtains or searching through catalogues, making little nasal humming noises as she worked. It was like an apiary in there. That continual buzzing was a torture. Please, I begged her, act like a woman, not a bee. With Stefan she either smothered him with love, hugged and kissed him until I told her she would soon rub his face off with all that kissing, or she forgot he was there. When she got on a cleaning jag or had one of her depressions, she was completely unaware of his existence. He could howl like a wolf. Nothing. The boy had a way of rubbing up against you like an eager little dog. It was all I could do not to smack him. One day I finally did.

We had gone out into the country for a picnic. Bucolic setting, rolling hills, green meadows sprinkled with wildflowers. There was even a horse. You should have seen my son. He took one look at that horse and he was off. He started speaking to him when he was already yards away. Hello you I'm Stefan and this kind of thing. When he got up close he reached out his little fingers to stroke the horse's muzzle. He must have frightened the creature, who promptly nipped him with his big yellow applecrunching teeth. It broke the skin. Right away Lena began to shriek like a lunatic. Stefan was screaming and holding out his hand as though it no longer belonged to him. We had to put up with this and far worse during the war my boy, I told him. This is a pleasure compared to what we went through. You would not have made it with all this screaming and crying. How about a little courage, a little bravery my little Jew. But the screaming went on and I slapped him.

———

For years he held it against me. Claimed he remembered everything. As soon as it happened he stopped crying and looked at me in shock. You monster, cried my wife, how could you, and she tried to beat at me with her fists. How I wish I had never laid eyes on you, she screamed. Compared to life with you, the ghetto was a funfair. Maybe I had gone too far. I held out my arms to him. But he refused absolutely to come near me and coldly, as though he were an adult and not a child, he turned away. And somewhere I was glad he was hardening up, learning, as I had to, to expect the worst. You're young. You probably want to have a child. Well don't look at me. Get yourself a nice young man who doesn't know what it's all about. I've had enough children by now. They are nothing but heartache. Like deep sea sponges. Sucking up love. So much need. Endless need. Love me, love me, love me. Exhausting. He poured himself a glass of brandy. Exhausting.

What happened, he said, is that Stefan did not make it. Did not make it? asked Kitty as though she had misunderstood. He got sick when he was thirteen. With pneumonia. Lena and I were already divorced. She hated me, but when this happened she called me. I got on a plane and flew to Vienna. She was waiting for me at the apartment. She had aged. Her hair was gray and there were rings around her neck and lines beside her eyes. I had never seen her so calm. He is going to die, she said to me. That was all. Then she turned around and walked away. I followed her. I remember she wore a baggy gray dress, not at all in fashion. She took me into his room. He was asleep. I watched him and I thought, Is this my son? This boy who is lying here with his white face. I wanted my son to be a hero. Not a sickly boy with a pale face. What a terrible disappointment. The next morning he was gone. They sat there without speaking. A large white paper flower with a yellow center which he kept on a shelf suddenly floated down. Kitty would have liked to pick it up and throw it away. It looked so dirty lying there. As though it had spent its life on the dustheap. Why do you keep this thing? she asked at last. Why does one keep anything? he replied.

With graceful fingers he lifted a toothpick from a small cardboard box and began to pry between his teeth. You should have seen me in those days, he told her. Vienna. Right after the war. How handsome I was. His eyes softened. Oh God did I have girlfriends. You look like a truck driver with that thing stuck in your mouth, she murmured. No sooner did one leave my bed than another one crawled in. One left her stockings behind and another one took them away. He spread out his hands and the toothpick jumped in his mouth. What could I do? That was no picnic trying to keep them apart. How hard did you try? asked Kitty. They all wanted me. The up-and-coming playwright. He got up and went to the freezer and pulled out a bottle of vodka. He raised the bottle. A little drop, my angel? She shook her head. He polished a small shot glass with his sleeve and sat down. At that time every girl in Vienna wanted to be an actress. That was the thing to be. They pinched their cheeks, tried to look well fed, and went to endless readings on cold stages. And then, he continued, they came back to slip under my eiderdown and tell me all about it.

He drank back the shot. His cheeks grew shiny. I remember Erika. She had a little hat with a flower. Like the twenties. Like my mother's generation. I couldn't resist that little hat. I saw her waiting for a bus (they never came in those days) and I brought her home with me that night. It was so cold the Danube was solid ice and the pigeons froze to the ledges. But my little Erika and I were cozy as two mice. She would clear her throat with a little scratching noise and look at me expectantly. And when I told her what to take off next she didn't hesitate. How cozy we were in my little bed under the eaves. Delicious. Yum yum. Why can't you wear a garter belt, he demanded suddenly, like the girls did in those days? He reached out a hand to her and she pulled away. Are you jealous, my darling? If you had been there I would have seduced you on the spot and dragged you home over my shoulder. What wouldn't we have done beneath that eiderdown? But you weren't born, my darling. You didn't even exist.

You're silent as a tomb, he complained. He pinched her cheek. I would have sat you on my lap, he crooned, and fed you hot chocolate mit schlag with a little spoon. And I would have bounced you up and down. We wouldn't have gotten out of bed for two weeks. Oh God, he moaned, if you knew what you do to me you whore of Babylon. The concierge was a Frau Kummel. With a sharp nose and a glass eye. Ach so many girls, she would say to me, it's not good for the reputation of the house. What reputation, Frau Kummel? I asked her. I should have taken the slut to bed to shut her up. But she was flat as a board with narrow shoulders. Not my type at all. She wore red slippers and three long sweaters at a time. She was thin as a rail. When my first play was produced she changed her tune. That's the Viennese concierge for you. Suddenly there is someone of renown in the house and she's all aflutter. He got up from the table and went to the chest of drawers in the corner. He tugged at one of the drawers, stuffed to the top with papers. He hauled up a box covered in peeling flowered paper. The box was filled with black-and-white photos. Look at me, he said proudly, holding out one of them. How you would have loved me then. Look at my dark curls. How slim I was. He sucked in his stomach. Look, he appealed to her. Like this. She studied the photo for a moment and put it down. Very nice, she said. Nice? he cried and took it from her hand. He stared at his own image. What I wouldn't give . . . he said quietly.

She pulled at a small snapshot and bent close to see. He sat in a darkened nightclub with a group of people, his arm around a smiling dark-haired woman. She had large eyes and full painted lips, and though she was smiling her eyes seemed lost in sadness. That was taken in The Red Feather. We used to go there around midnight. That's when it got really lively. All the theater people, the writers and the artists used to go there. Our favorite waiter was named Adolf and we ragged him mercilessly. Thanks for the memories Adolf, we would say on the way out. Bergen-Belsen was as much fun as we ever had. The poor man, tall and thin with a long quivering straw-colored mustache, would hold up his hands and beg us to stop. But that only encouraged us. I drank like a fish in those days. Thanks for the holiday camp at Sobibor, I would call out. He peered into the photo. Oh yes. Elke. Why aren't you smiling? asked Kitty. I look ugly with my mouth open, he informed her. He was pulling this Elke against him, his fingers pressing into the flesh of her bare arm. Why is she so sad? she asked. She's not sad, he cried looking down at the photo. She's in love. She was mad about me. But she looks far away. She wasn't far away at all, he said with disgust. She's lovesick. Kitty looked into the woman's eyes. Where was she from? Bucharest, he answered. She spent the war in a pitch-black coal cellar. It so happened it belonged to an old peasant who made his drunken way down the cellar stairs several nights a week stinking of vodka. He shrugged. What could she do? She didn't want to be denounced.

When she came out at last at the end of the war she couldn't see for a week. Meanwhile her whole family had disappeared. He sucked on his cigarette. Sad? he asked. What is sad. We're alive. Suddenly he looked at her and smiled. That Elke was really something in bed. I don't want to hear, she said sharply. There wasn't anything she wouldn't try. Those were the days, he said. When I was still young. And now? she asked, wounded. He shrugged. Now is now. He sat down wearily. We had lived through a war, he told her. You can't understand. You didn't know whether you would be alive from one moment to the next. So you fucked like a rabbit because it might be the last time. We're not talking about puritan morality, he said to her. We're talking about the condemned man's last meal.

Look at this, he said, a special facsimile edition of *The Chimney Sweep* with my notes and changes in the margins reproduced. I remember the man who played the lead. Ezra was his name. Ezra Rosensweig. He came to audition. Into the theater walked this man with shaved head, a broken nose and eyes full of hatred. He was dressed in an ill-fitting overcoat and dusty shoes, looking like he hadn't eaten for a week. I couldn't believe my eyes. Exactly who I had imagined for the role of this man who performs an unspeakable task. This man was so sullen, so full of rage that I was afraid it would all implode. But once he was onstage the effect was extraordinary. During rehearsals he drew people from every corner of the theater. Frau Baumgarten who took care of the dressing rooms and the lavatories for the first time came up from her subterranean precincts and stood in the aisle, her little eyes glistening like a crow's. I had expected him to rant and rave. He did neither. He spoke in a quiet voice so pitiless that all human hope and warmth had long since been abandoned. I was beside myself with excitement. For six months Ezra went on six nights a week. We were sold out months in advance. The reviews were incredible. They called me a master, a genius, a wizard, God knows what else. He reminded me of myself, this Ezra. When he spoke the words I had written, I felt as though I had spoken them myself.

Ezra began to spend all his time at the theater. He would arrive earlier and earlier. Frau Baumgarten told me about it. A strange fire took hold of him. His eyes grew almost feverish, his performances became more and more extraordinary, more and more frightening. Six months, night after night. He had a girl whom he kept in his apartment, a skinny waif with pale sickly skin and a ragged woolen scarf tied around her neck. I saw her once. He spoke of her as though she were of no consequence. He referred to her as the girl.

The last performance was to be on New Year's Eve. This was in 1956. A champagne party was planned for afterwards at Gartner's Restaurant. There was a standing ovation at the end of the last performance that must have lasted for fifteen minutes. Ezra stood there onstage expressionless, motionless. The stage lights caused his eyes to sink into deep shadows and accentuate his cheekbones. And then at last he walked off. Go ahead, he told us, I'll join you there in a few minutes. I was against it but the others said leave him, he needs a few minutes on his own. So we left. After half an hour he still hadn't come. So someone went back to see what was keeping him. We had just been told he had won the Friedrich Heinz Blessing Award for the best performance of 1956. Well of course you know what had happened. He had hanged himself.

———

He left a note for the girl he lived with. As it turned out, they were married. They even had a small child. All that time together and he never told me he had a baby or what the woman meant to him. It was all in the letter. *The Chimney Sweep* was put on in Berlin, London, New York, Tel Aviv. Many years later the woman got in touch with me. Her name was Saskia. She had become a well-known sculptor. She was middle-aged by then but still with the same childlike quality. She told me about him, about their life together and her life since. She never remarried. The child, a girl, was an actress. Ezra, she told me, had been a member of the Sonderkommando during the war, had worked the chimneys, as she put it. This also he never said a word about. If I had known I would not have allowed him to play the part. But I didn't know. He never mentioned a word about the war. Joseph poured himself a drink. If you do it right, he said, a play is as alive as a life. The man survived everything. And then a play brought him down. What is the sense of it? He had lines around his eyes, she saw. His mouth drooped. Kitty was silent. How about something to eat? he asked her.

———

Do you know what they said about me? The major post-war playwright in the German language. Heir to Kafka. Have I told you about the opening night of *Sticks and Stones*? I was the most important man in Vienna that night. Everyone came. The mayor. Marlene Dietrich was in town and came with Erich Maria Remarque. The theater had been sold out for weeks. Tickets were being sold on the black market for a fortune. I stood at the back smoking a cigarette. The lights went down. Onstage, out of the darkness emerges the outline of a small cupboard. And in this doll-sized cupboard a man is folded up. When the music starts up, a faint blue light comes up and he unfolds himself with difficulty and steps out with a little suitcase. Total silence. I did not dare to breathe.

Halfway through Act One an older Viennese gentleman walked out angrily. Schrecklich, he muttered on the way out. What a disgrace. I followed him out to the lobby. The man was sputtering. He wore an expensive camel's hair coat. My dear sir, I began with the utmost courtesy, it seems I have offended you. But it was not so long ago that you too offended me. And I, dear sir, could not walk out. He was livid. I have nothing further to say to you, young man, he shouted. When I crept back into the theater there was still the silence of the tomb. They were riveted. It was the moment when he lifts up her skirt with his cane and remarks that soon they will be overrunning Poland. It was all I could do not to laugh out loud. I was alive. And my play was packing them in. Can you understand what that was? First they want you dead. Then they raise you up to the stature of a god. You don't know whether you're coming or going.

He tilted his coffee cup and stared into it. Strange coincidence. The same night the play opened my second wife, Lena, gave birth to Stefan. When the curtain came down he was already in this world. Another Jew about to face an uncertain future. But I could not be there. Not yet. I had to attend the opening-night party. In the morning with a terrible hangover I went off to the hospital with a box of chocolate-covered cherries. My wife was already talking circumcision, crazy woman. I ranted and raved until they were ready to throw me out of the hospital. I should mark my son for extermination? he asked incredulously. I went back to Dalya's that afternoon. You remember Dalya? She was the love of my life. After a bout of lovemaking she calmed me down. Told me not to be a fool and to go and have the child circumcised. The war is over, she said. I wasn't convinced. But Dalya had been in a camp and if she said the war was over, maybe it was. She could convince me of anything, that Dalya. A real Polish Jewish beauty. Thick burnished copper hair and freckles. As warm and welcoming as sunlight. And skin as pale as milk. So thanks to Dalya my son was circumcised.

She had bought all the papers and we lay in bed and drank champagne and toasted my son and my play. I made her read the reviews out loud. She kept changing the words. How we laughed. Dalya. I was madly in love with her. Three years later she was dead. Drowned herself in the sea off Haifa. What a beauty. But what nightmares. She cried out, she tore at her face, she awoke wide-eyed with terror which no embrace could wipe away. Why did she die? Who knows. To stop the nightmares. To sleep peacefully at last. Nothing, he said, will ever be the same again. He rolled a cigarette and licked slowly at the seam. At least she died in Israel. Eretz Israel.

One cold night, he began, moving the tobacco onto the thin white sheet, my sweetheart went out to work and I sat down at the table in the corner and stayed up all night writing *The Way Down*. Kitty nodded in recognition. He rolled the cigarette between his fingers, his fingertips pointed and alert like a man reading the Torah. I didn't stop once. The words poured out of my head until I was dizzy. He filled his glass and held the bottle out to her. She shook her head. How many words a Jew can stuff in his head. The whole world flies up into his head. All the years of the war they were collecting up there, an infinite number of words to describe what had happened. Only when it came to describing, the words turned out to be useless. Water and dust. He lit his cigarette and the paper crackled. Nevertheless something had collected up there and in that cold little room the letters rolled out like from a bag of beads.

I wanted to read it to my sweetheart when she came back that night but my little sparrow was so exhausted she fell into bed. He pulled a clove of tobacco from his tongue. But I read it to her the next morning as she rubbed her eyes and pulled at her slip. And she laughed. Imagine that. I don't think she understood a word. You remember, he asked Kitty, when Stanislas says listen to the vultures singing in the trees, it's such a familiar tune a passerby could almost sing along? She nodded. Oh she laughed her head off at that. Said it was cute. He shook his head wryly. What could

I do but pinch the silly girl's cheek. His voice rose. The book they later called the most important of the decade. The smoke floated up before him. There were furrows at the corners of his eyes. Thirty years ago. He looked at her sardonically. You were just learning how to spell, my angel. He shook his head. Those were the days. He threw back the schnapps and leaned toward her. The greatest postwar writer of them all. That's what they called me. *The Way Down* made me famous overnight. All the leading newspapers reviewed it. Vienna, Berlin, Frankfurt, Prague. You should see the folders of clippings. Bitter brew, he said quietly. That's what they called it in the papers. Black as the ace of spades. What were they expecting? He poured out another schnapps. No one cared. Everything had happened and no one cared. As though it were already past and forgotten. Only we couldn't forget. There wasn't a moment when we could forget. Except between the warm thighs of a woman. And not even then. Kitty reached out a hand to him across the table. What is this? he asked. Comfort? You want to comfort me? She pulled her hand back and cradled it in the other hand. Do you think you can comfort me? he asked incredulous. Kitty flushed. No, she said.

———

Out the window snow flurries are blown in furious circles by the wind. From the squat chimney of a small house a plume of smoke rises. She imagines an old couple from a fairy tale inside, each drawing in on a briar pipe, awaiting the visit of a magical animal. But beyond the cozy warmth of that cottage the land stretches white and barren. Beneath that frozen ground Joseph will lie. Who will say kaddish for him? Both his sons are dead. Who will recite the prayer of remembrance, a prayer so ancient it was formulated in Aramaic. This time it is at an end. This time he will not be reprieved. His many lives have been used up.

I had more lives then than a cat, he told her. Does a cat have nine? I had many more. He lifted his white handkerchief and blew loudly. Why I don't know. What had I done to deserve it? It certainly was not for my good deeds or my pure and blameless heart. But so it goes. One night in Amsterdam, he began, tucking his handkerchief back into the sagging pocket of his robe, I hurried down the street, as fast as one can move without running. It was deathly cold and there were no lights but the light of the frigid moon. I had stayed out past curfew and the dark streets were deserted. I cursed Marijke. Five more minutes, my sweetheart had murmured, pressing her soft breasts against me. What could

I do? Well, I thought, my teeth chattering with cold, I am the last Jew left on the face of the earth. I had seen the others leaving, dragging their useless suitcases, struggling to close their coats. I remember still the misery in their eyes.

As it turned out I was only the second to the last. I heard the sound of boots on the cobblestones and a sudden shout. I repeated to myself my Dutch name, my Dutch date of birth as I looked up at the moon whose white face shone brightly among the cold stars. There were three of them in black uniform, their well-fed faces red with cold. Eat, he said to her pointing at the chipped plate of meats, now that you have the chance. It wasn't so long ago that the Germans rounded up all that was pleasurable and valuable in this world for themselves. Caviar, diamonds, tobacco, cars, gasoline, gold, meat, butter, sugar, coffee, and tea. And they had no desire to share.

Quickly I pulled my false papers out from those pants Marijke had so recently unbuttoned. They asked me where I had been and where I was going. But there was a Dutch Nazi with them and he couldn't place my accent. I told him the usual story about my Austrian mother, but he wasn't impressed. It was bitterly cold. They were shivering and I felt that they blamed me for their discomfort. They ordered me to drop my pants. What could I do? I began to undo my belt. Hurry up, they ordered me, poking their guns at me. The Dutchman shouted more than the other two put together until they told him to calm down and not give himself a heart attack. He spread a slice of rye bread with liverwurst and held it out to her. You don't eat?

At that moment, with my hand on my zipper, three shots rang out. They forgot about me and began to run toward the sound. I stood there in the cold trying to refasten my belt but it seemed my fingers had frozen. I made my way back to my attic room in a daze. It appeared I was still alive. Later I learned that a Jew had been shot. I tried to find out who he was, but no one seemed to know. I went back the next morning and passed back and forth through the same streets but there was no trace of him. This was the beginning of my belief in luck. Why him and not me? He shrugged. Maybe he was a saint and I was Barrabas, released in his place. He chewed slowly. It is all luck. Never mind brains or beauty or a good heart. In the end it was all luck. Remember that my sweetheart.

———

She asked Henri once what he thought about the notion of luck. He called it irrational. He believed in talent and hard work. When I draw plans for a building, he said, I think of every eventuality: heat, cold, earthquakes, everything. No one can think of every eventuality, she told him. Not even a good architect. That mollified him. Every eventuality, Joseph would have said mockingly, you are lucky if you think of one. And whichever one you think of, there's one you forgot. You anticipate everything and then the sun forgets to rise in the morning. You anticipate everything and the cat runs away with the map.

We celebrated my latest piece of luck in bed, Marijke and me. You, I told her, are my biggest piece of luck. How did God create an angel like that? She taught me songs from the North, strange melodies in northern dialect. I still remember them. She had pink slippers with pom-poms on them which came from France and she had covered the walls of her tiny room with pages torn from French film magazines. As we made love on her noisy bed Jean Gabin,

Edwige Feuillère, and Michelle Morgan looked down at us. Stop, said Kitty. He shook his head. So jealous. I am speaking of a girl I have not seen since 1945. He balanced his lighter carefully on the slope of the sugar bowl. She slept with men for money. What could I do? I wasn't her first and I wouldn't be her last. But I was the one she loved. I don't want to hear any more, protested Kitty. She saved my life, he replied looking out at her from under heavy lids. Does that mean nothing to you? She gave me the money for my false papers. Without them I would have disappeared along with everyone else. He smoked quietly. My grandfather in his caftan should only have known who saved his grandson's life. Besides, this girl of whom you are so jealous has been dead for nearly fifty years. Do you think that sleeping with the enemy went unpunished at the end of the war? Far from it.

Do you think, Kitty asked him once, that you are the only one to have lovers? I too have had lovers. He looked up quickly. Not too many, I hope. Quite a few, she replied. Shall I tell you about them? No, my sweetheart, I'm far too jealous.

———

He collected the loose tobacco and herded it into his small metal box. That was not the only time I was reprieved. One night we stood huddled in an air-raid shelter, packed in like the geese of the goyim on the way to market. Which is to say without a cubic centimeter between us. And I thought I must separate myself from these people. There was no safety in numbers as far as I was concerned. On the contrary. I could think better on my own. So I began to push my way out. They shouted at me to stop, motherly arms reached out to bar my way. Stay, they urged me. But I would as soon have stayed in a burning building. In that crowd I was helpless. I struggled out into the air. It was a clear night, ideal for bombing. I looked up and saw the myriad stars spread out across the night sky. I thought of my grandfather proudly leading his geese to market on foot. And his disdain for the goyim who crammed them into cages on the backs of carts where they could barely breathe. There was utter silence and then a thunderous explosion. I fell to the ground. When I got up, I saw that the entire shelter and everyone in it was gone. Only I was left standing. My grandfather might have patted me on the head and called me a clever Jew. Whether I was or not I set out to find myself a woman, any woman. I wanted to celebrate my survival on this black and bitter earth of ours.

I found her wandering on the road, a woman of about thirty. Her dress was torn and her eyes empty. Hey, I called out to her. We're still alive. She looked at me unseeing. Why shouldn't we celebrate? She had no reaction to this idea but when I put my arm around her she didn't stop me. There was no warmth there at all. Her shoulder was cold and dead and I almost gave up then and there. But it doesn't take long to warm up a woman, any woman. And before long we lay down together by the side of the road. Kitty poured out more tea. It seems so bleak, she said, so inhuman. He scratched at his chest. How little you understand, he replied.

He drank, his eyes half shut. There is nothing like Dutch women. Lusty and horny in all kinds of weather. And how they love to laugh. Did you know that when a woman's eyes glisten with desire they call it zaad vragende ogen, sperm demanding eyes. Only the Dutch women train their little dogs to lick them between the legs. Kuttelikker they call them. How can you not love women like this? Made

for bed. He put down his cup and studied her. Like you my
darling with your sperm producing eyes. Come to me. Sit
on my lap. I want to feel you. Kitty shook her head with a
smile. Shall I come and get you? he asked. Is that what you
want? He stood up and thrust out his large chest. What a
sexy girl you are. Why have you come to me?

I think, said Kitty resolutely one morning, you should
open the shutters. It's so dark in here. At the far end of the
room, she reached out a hand for the clasp. Leave them
closed, he ordered her harshly, rolling a slice of salami between his fingers. I have seen quite enough as it is. Just for
a few minutes, Kitty suggested, to let in a little light. God
forbid, he replied. He pressed the roll into his mouth.
Once a woman came and threw open the shutters and
started cleaning the place from top to bottom. He licked
the grease off his fingers. She had beautiful red hair but I
had to get rid of her. There is nothing for me to see out
there. He tapped his head. It's all in here. You are still a
young girl. Just starting out. You are looking for sunlight
and flowers and all the delicious and unknown adventures
that might befall you in the great wide world. But I have
had enough adventures by now. More than enough. So
leave the shutters alone. Otherwise, he said shaking his

finger with mock severity, I shall have to get rid of you too. You wouldn't, said Kitty lightly. No, he sighed. How could I? You make it sound, said Kitty, as though nothing more could happen to you. Please God, he replied. She shook her head. I can't understand. No, he agreed, of course you can't.

The train stops in Brussels. Looking out Kitty sees a couple embracing on the platform. Every time the woman tries to pull away, they look at each other one last time and embrace again. Both wear down coats so their embrace is puffy and shapeless, their heads small and sharply defined. Three boys with shaved skulls, chained boots and tattoos pass them and seeing the embrace spit with disdain. In their hard new world, Kitty imagines, no embraces, just the tough love of the new order. The whistle blows. The woman grabs her bag and they kiss one last time. Kitty looks away. You and your girlish romantic fantasies, Joseph taunted her. All hearts and flowers. What do you know of real life?

The doors open and a blast of freezing air enters the car. A line of people in heavy boots, bundled into coats and parkas, carrying their luggage, board the train. Kitty sits in an aisle seat. So far she has been lucky, no one is sitting beside her. So she can look out the window and watch the landscape pass by. But now a young woman breathing heavily and dragging a large suitcase behind her comes down the aisle. She asks Kitty whether the seat next to her is free. No, answers Kitty right away. Across the aisle the old French woman with the pointed nose starts indignantly. How does she dare? she hisses. Go ahead and sit down mademoiselle, that seat is not taken. Kitty stares out the window. The flat fields rush by. The young woman hesitates but in a moment she continues on down the aisle. Kitty smiles to herself and prepares for battle. Joseph would already have spoken up. Don't be such a good girl, he would tell her. So upright, so honest, so well mannered. Is that a way to live? Only in peacetime, in a well-to-do family, does one have this luxury. How long would you have survived the war, with all your exquisite manners? Oh no, please, I beg of you, he would say mockingly. You have the bread. I'll wait. Mind your own business, she will say to the woman. Or should she add old bag. They could have used you, she will say, under Communism. What a nerve, says the old woman to a stranger next to her. Can you imag-

ine? Saying the seat is taken when it's free? What an out-
rage. Kitty waits, but the woman does not confront her.
She cannot lose sight of the frozen fields, the cool white
disk of the moon. The train begins to move. Soon they
will be in Holland.

On the table was a bowl of lemons, dry and wrinkled,
without juice, turned a dusky orange from having sat on
the radiator for so long. Kitty examined them with dis-
taste. Why do you keep those dried-out lemons? she
asked. Like something left over from your grandmother's
time. Have some, said Joseph, pouring out the schnapps
until it overflowed the glasses. It softens even the hardest
hearts. Are you speaking of mine? asked Kitty in astonishment. No, my darling, he replied, I am speaking of mine.
He clinked his glass briefly against hers. What are we celebrating? asked Kitty. We are alive, replied Joseph. Reason
enough to celebrate. He put back his head and drank
down the schnapps. Shall we get up and dance like the
Hasids? No, not necessary. We'll drink to survival. That's
enough. You should have seen how they danced in Palestine after the war, those who weren't too tired to move.
Leaping and kicking like the cossacks used to do. Night af-

ter night. When a woman has been dancing for hours, you can do what you like with her. All her female hormones are in an uproar. He raised a warning finger. You must just remember in the heat of the moment not to let her propose marriage.

I was married twice. And that is more than enough for any man. The man who marries might as well put on a cap and bells, that's how big a fool he is. He dropped shreds of tobacco onto the paper and rolled it. Women are endlessly unhappy in marriage. I learned this first at home. Often when it grew dark I would find my mother seated at the kitchen table, the chopping board before her, the knife held motionless and forgotten in her hand. What is it, Mama? I would ask her. Her pale blue eyes would fill with tears. Shall I hold the knife for you Mama, while you cry? I asked her. But she shook her head and put it down on the table where the blade gleamed. I knew why she was crying. She didn't have to tell me. It was because her husband was never at home. And for this there is no comfort. I read her the stories I had written. About clowns and dwarfs and a little boy who disappears down a hole. Don't forget dinner, I prompted her and she would motion to the stove where Mitzi had left a pan of meat and gravy. I tried magic tricks, card tricks, I told her my best jokes. Nothing helped.

Sometimes I stared at the starburst pattern on one of her silk dresses and imagined another galaxy where dogs walked on their hind legs and carried cameras around their necks. Mama, I said, let's pretend we're going on a trip. But she didn't want to play. Night after night we sat there the two of us as I crashed two little trains together and she wiped at her eyes. Sometimes when she wasn't feeling too sad she called me her sweetheart and her little love and her handsome boy and predicted that one day I would win the Nobel Prize. I blamed the matchmaker. She had made a terrible mistake. She had matched two people who were oil and water.

Imagine, my mother would say to me, in springtime the snow melts, the mud dries up, and the meadows come into bloom. She was talking about her shtetele in the Ukraine. The brooks start to move once again and the water is as clear and fresh as a mountain spring. You can lie down in the sweet grasses and look up at the sky and see a herd of white clouds moving across the blue sky. And the black cherries. The raspberries. And she would lift her shoulders slightly to indicate their incredible sweetness. When my parents told me we were packing up and going to Vienna, she said, I did not want to go. And on the day of departure I hid at the top of a neighbor's barn beneath the hay.

They brought the shtetl with them, my mother and her parents. My grandfather refused to learn German, to wear a suit. He never left the confines of his own neighborhood. My grandmother still wore her country wig and old-fashioned shoes. My grandfather had left his geese behind but he soon found the nearest thing. He opened a tiny shop where he sold goose down. In that small space stood wooden barrels filled to the brim with seven kinds of goose down. The women came in with quilt covers and pillowcases and filled them with feathers. Once a woman came in and she sneezed. Not once but five times. My grandfather invoked the name of the Almighty. The feathers blew out of their barrels and flew around the tiny shop as though on their own steam. How I wish I had been there, said Joseph with yearning. Imagine the fun. When my mother married, her dowry was goose feathers. Eiderdowns and pillows, all filled with the finest Hungarian goose feathers.

A few months after they arrived in Vienna my mother's mother died. My mother became servant and companion to her father. She cooked for him, cleaned for him, dusted his prayer books. He even required her to comb his long beard for him. She was forbidden to speak to boys. She wrote poems in small flowered notebooks and hid them in her drawer. Poems about flowers and brooks and love and all the dreams tucked away in a young girl's heart. She wrote them in German. Even if her father had discovered them, he wouldn't have been able to read them. He knew only the Yiddish alphabet. When she married, she brought her notebooks with her and hid them again.

My mother was twenty-six, already a spinster in those days, when he died. But at last a match was found for her. If her parents had still been alive, it would have been unthinkable. He was not an observant Jew. Far from it. He

observed nothing at all. And my mother came from a religious family. Not only was my father not religious, he
forbade my mother to act, as he put it, like an ignorant
shtetl girl. A handsome man, whispered the matchmaker,
elegant. He knows how old you are and he accepts it.
What a find. A salesman, she added. The matchmaker was
right. But she forgot to mention how experienced he was
with women. They met. It was true, my mother told me,
he was very handsome with his wavy hair parted down
the center. She liked his coolness. He didn't push her.
This reassured her. She wasn't used to men, except her father, and didn't want one who would overwhelm her. She
told me this. It was only later, when it was too late, that
she understood. What she had taken for gentlemanly re-
serve was in fact indifference. He shook his head. My
poor mother. She deserved better than she got.

Sometimes my father didn't come home for months at a
time. Money ran low and we had to cut back. But when he
was expected, the house was cleaned from top to bottom,
his collars washed and starched, the most expensive cuts
of veal ordered, and my mother put on her best dress, the
black one with the lace sleeves. I was told to brush my
hair carefully and bring out my last report card from

school. Your father, my cousin informed me years later, was a real ladies' man. He had women all over the place. Like a pasha. Out of his brown leather sample case he sold them ribbons and stockings and embroidered hand-kerchiefs. All manner of feminine frills and fluff. They fell for him one after the other. Meanwhile my mother and I stayed at home and drank endless cups of tea together at the kitchen table. Once in a while she read me her flow-ery poems. Someday, I thought, I too will be out on the road, with many women and a carefree salesman's heart.

My father wore well-cut suits and a flower in his button-hole. And he sang songs from operettas. He was a sales-man after all. But sometimes when he was ready to go out the door on one of his long trips he flew into a rage. He couldn't find his sample case, or his gloves or his hat. And we had to run all over looking for them while he shouted that he would never come back to this household where nothing could ever be found.

Joseph rolled a cigarette and lit it. She was too timid, too soft, he said angrily. Why didn't she stand up for herself? When we went to the store she allowed everyone to push

ahead. And before anyone in uniform, even if he were the
man from the gasworks come to read the meter, she became flushed and obsequious. The smoke rose in spirals.
But I will tell you something strange. According to my
cousin, at the end another side of her emerged. And he, my
devil-may-care father, became listless and withdrawn. It is
all madness. What axis does the world turn on? None at all.
At any moment it can turn upside down and inside out.
Can and does. Still my father was full of fun when he wasn't
in a rage about one thing or another. He loved jokes and
magicians. And he had seen the most famous magician in
all of Europe the year before I was born. Joseph got up and
went to put the kettle on and brought back a box of cookies. Take one, he said, holding out the box with a crushed
end. She dug in and pulled out a sugary crescent. I ate them
when I was a child, he told her. I found these in a shop
downtown. Soft and sweet and sprinkled with sugar. Just
like in the old days. Take another.

Joseph chewed happily and the powdered sugar fell on
his chin. It was in 1926. My father was in Budapest on
business. He heard by chance that S, the greatest magician in all of Europe, was to give a performance that very

night. He went to the theater where S was to appear and managed to get one of the last seats. The theater was full to bursting. The show was to begin at eight. It was a hot night and the women fanned themselves in their seats. The crowd waited. Patiently at first. But time passed and he did not come. They looked at their watches every few moments and still he did not appear. Finally at ten to nine the curtain parted and the magician himself stepped out on the stage. Good evening ladies and gentlemen, he said with a bow. I apologize to you for being five minutes late. At once everyone consulted their watches. Every watch in the house said 8:05. Joseph drank his coffee. A great wizard, he remarked. A Jew of course.

My father knew hundreds of jokes. And he remembered them all. But his favorite was Lenin in Poland. When he told this joke at the table when my uncles were there, extra water had to be poured into their glasses. I couldn't understand the joke at the time. And when I asked what it meant they laughed even louder. But I remembered the joke and a few years later in Amsterdam, it suddenly became clear.

———

Well, come on, urged Kitty, what's the joke? Which joke, my sweetheart? The Lenin in Poland joke. The Lenin in Poland joke? Do you mean to tell me you've never heard it? he asked in mock astonishment. She smiled. Would you like to hear it? She nodded. Today? Or shall we wait until tomorrow? He reached over and pinched her cheek. All right, all right. One day the news came that Lenin would be making a visit to Poland. What could they do for the great man? A delegation convened and they decided to commission a painting, a large and glorious oil painting on the theme "Lenin in Poland." Kitty lifted an orange from the bowl and began to peel it. They went to the town's master painter. He promised to have it ready in a month. After a month they returned but he put them off. Two weeks later they were back. He needed still more time. But at last, just one day before Lenin's arrival they went to the studio. As they stood there the painter pulled back the cloth from the enormous canvas. They gazed in shocked silence. In the painting they saw Trotsky climbing into bed with Lenin's wife. At last one of the delegation spoke up. But where is Lenin? Ah, replied the painter. Lenin is in Poland.

I imagined him telling that joke to his women as he sold them a pink satin stocking case or three yards of black lace. How they must have laughed together. And now, said Kitty, you tell it to your women. I never thought of that, he said in surprise. Kitty shrugged. My darling, he said to her, how clever you are. I don't deserve such a clever woman.

Kitty bites into a little cake. The crumbs fall on her black coat and she brushes them off. Suddenly she does not believe he is dead. He will be sitting in the front row of the synagogue with his wild hair flying out, the shirt button over his stomach unbuttoned, looking out at her slyly. Well my darling, he will say, what do you think of my little ruse? Listen, he will whisper, have I told you the one about Lenin in Poland? And he will pinch her cheek and take her to bed. He too is a great magician.

It is all theater, he told her. No need to be so earnest. One pretends to love, one pretends to hate, one plays at laughing, at crying. And meanwhile the actor rehearses in his mind his next emotion, his next impersonation. He lowered his voice and leaned close to her. You see, my angel, he must pretend he is alive. You should have been an actor, Kitty told him once. He regarded her with astonishment. But my sweet angel, my darling love, what else have I ever been?

In the photos he showed her he was always apart, alone in the midst of the others, unsmiling, staring into the camera, his shoulders held back as though he had been ordered to do so. In the wedding photo of him and Lena, his second wife, he does not even touch her. She wears a light-colored dress and holds a small bouquet. He, again unsmiling, wears a dark suit with the tie loosened. They do not appear to know each other. She might have been a woman passing in the street who had been asked to pose with him. Kitty cannot blame it on the war. It is a vast solitude that no one can enter, not even the women who clung to him, who opened themselves to him, who loved him. In the photo the bride looks dismayed. As though she has already understood that she has married a man who isn't there.

My parents, volunteered Kitty, were in Amsterdam in February of 1940. The canals were frozen, my mother

said, your father bought a hat, we got to the pier four
hours early. We were afraid to be late for the ship's sailing.
But in his nervousness, your father had bought a hat that
was far too large, and he left it on the dock. As we sailed,
standing at the railing to see the last of Europe, your father's new hat was lifted up by a gust of wind and spun in
the air above the water. I began to laugh, my mother said,
until the tears rolled down my cheeks. It dipped and flew
until at last it dropped to the waves and bobbed there, a
fine felt European hat that didn't fit. Everyone on the ship
spoke German. But no one wanted to speak about Germany. I don't remember Amsterdam, her mother had said,
running her fingers through her dark hair. It was all a blur.
I could only think, We mustn't miss the ship. They sailed
away, said Joseph bitterly. And left us behind. But they
didn't know, cried Kitty. You silly girl, replied Joseph,
brushing ashes off his striped robe, I'm not talking about
your decent upright parents and their new hat.

That night they heard the wind gusting. The shutters rat-
tled and creaked and sometime after midnight there was the
sound of screeching brakes far below and the crash of col-
liding metal. Too many cars, said Joseph lying beside her.
Everyone should ride bikes like they did during the war.

———

Except the Jews. The Jews were forbidden to ride bikes. That was how it began. Forbidden to go to the cinema, to walk in the park, to take the tram. And it got worse. One by one the right to live as the others lived narrowed and narrowed until one lost the right to live at all. Dalya, light of my life, told me about the sign posted above the gates of the Vilna ghetto: Attention. Jewish Quarter. Danger of contagion. Non-Jews forbidden to enter. Forbidden for Jews to look out the windows overlooking the street outside the ghetto. These windows must be completely camouflaged with paper and paint. Forbidden for Jews to speak German. Forbidden for Jews to discuss politics. Any Jew who speaks to or has relations with a non-Jew will be shot. Forbidden for Jews to consume fats. Forbidden for Jewish women to dye their hair or wear lipstick. Forbidden to pray. Forbidden to study. From the age of six all Jews must wear the yellow star inside and outside the ghetto. One must take off one's hat to every German who enters the ghetto. Forbidden to give birth. Women who give birth will be killed along with their baby. Kitty sat motionless, her eyes on the table. What's the matter, darling, he said, watching her. Don't be sad. We're alive, aren't we? That's what counts. Kitty began

to cry, wiping her eyes with her fingers. Don't cry, my angel, he said lightly. He began to hum. Please my sweetheart. He put his arm around her and stroked her cheek.
Don't cry my angel, he said. It's no good crying. It won't get
us home any faster. Never mind the war. We won't talk
about the war anymore. Not if it makes you cry. He pressed
her head against him. Shh, he murmured. I would cry too if
I could.

Out the window the sky is darkening over the fields of
Holland. In the distance on a broad stretch of icy river
they are skating, bundled into dark clothes, woolen
scarves knotted around their heads as they glide over the
ice, doll-like figures beneath the enormity of the sky. The
food cart is coming down the aisle, the bottles clinking,
the boxed nuts shaking. Kitty buys two small bottles of
red wine. It's cold, she explains to the young boy with a
smile. He nods eagerly, his lips red, his hair cut so close it
is like stubble. Snowstorm in Amsterdam, he informs her.
We could be delayed. Delayed? What if she has traveled
through this frozen landscape for nothing. He counts out
the change carefully with moist hands whose nails have
been bitten down to the quick. He leans against the cart

and it rolls past. Kitty unscrews a bottletop and pours out
the red wine.

At night he cried out, rocking in the tangled white sheets.
No, he would cry, his arms flailing, can't, won't, and open
his eyes in terror. Kitty felt her heart beating as she shook
him awake. You're safe, she told him urgently, it's all right.
He was bathed in sweat. I was put into a little paper boat, he
said breathlessly, a paper hat on my head. Like Moses'
mother, my own mother set the little boat into the water
and kissed me on the forehead. I held on to her with both
hands but she pried open my fingers and gave the boat a
push. The boat was so light that it pitched and rocked in
the calm water. I looked back at my mother angrily. Why?
I called out. What have I done? She put a finger to her lips
and soon I could no longer see her. Night came, the current
picked up, and my boat fell down a swiftly flowing water-
fall. At the bottom I heard a murmuring as though I were in
synagogue. I tried to stay upright as my paper boat shud-
dered. And everywhere in the darkness were the discarded
suitcases of the dead. He grabbed her hand. She wanted to
get rid of me, he hissed. Kitty stroked his wet face. How
can you say that? she whispered to him in the darkness. She
wanted you to live.

———

She felt his wavy hair against her face, the pungent smell at the roots. His cheekbone lay painfully against hers. She was pressed up against his chest, sleek with sweat, so close to him that she felt his heart, heard the sound of his breath in her ears. Let's stay like this, he murmured, his arms tight around her. Stay just this close to me. A woman lay like this once. On a train from Berlin to Vienna. Lay so close to me I heard the thoughts in her brain. And the feelings in her heart. Suddenly he opened his eyes wide and looked at her accusingly. Were you watching me as I slept? Oh Joseph, said Kitty, I was asleep myself. He held tightly to her arm. This is how Lilith enters into the dreams of men and destroys them. She sucks out their virility and turns them frightened and useless. Like an eggsucker sucks the egg out through a pinprick in the shell, Lilith needs only the most microscopic opening to empty you out. One must be on one's guard all the time. She comes in all disguises. Yours for example. Me? asked Kitty groggily. I'm not Lilith. What do you call yourself if not the Queen of Demons, the High Demoness herself. Then he smiled at her stricken voice and pinched her cheek. All right, all right, he said, his voice still thick with sleep. Maybe you're only Lilith's assistant.

And tugging at the sheets, he turned over so that his back was to her.

The train stops unexpectedly and Kitty looks out. The snow has settled on the branches of the trees and coated the roofs. A white rabbit camouflaged by its coat emerges, its nose twitching, its paws laid against the snow. Shall I tell you about my first dream in Eretz Israel? he asked her. I had reached the Holy Land. The dream of my Zionist parents, to come at last to the Land that God had promised to us all those years ago. And now I was here. I slept and in my dream an angel hovered above me. Go to the land where I will tell you, she whispered to me, this messenger of God. But I am here, I told her in confusion. I have arrived. She lifted her white skirt and I saw the sturdy legs of Mitzi, my nurse in Vienna, and the thick white country stockings she wore. But she had no shoes and I called out to her and pointed to her feet. If you don't put on your shoes I said to her in German, we will never reach the Holy Land. My first dream in the Land of Israel. But I soon awoke. He gathered her up in his arms and holding her hips he entered her with a groan. Afterward she began to stroke his shoulder. He grew rigid. Stop that, he said tightly. I cannot bear to be stroked.

One night Joseph stood before the stove in his striped robe and backless yellow slippers frying eggs. He set them down over hard bread and the pale yolks broke and ran out on the plates. Look how delicious, he said to her. During the war you were shot for stealing an egg. Never mind. Eat up. He cut eagerly through the bread with knife and fork. As he pressed the large square into his mouth, glistening yellow threads ran down his chin. He ate with relish. I'm afraid, he said at last, that I'm becoming too attached to you. Too attached to those green eyes and white bottom. Kitty paused, her knife and fork raised. And that's no good, he went on, forking egg into his mouth. But Joseph, said Kitty quietly, what's wrong with that? Isn't that what happens? He ate rapidly. During the war those with attachments made fatal mistakes. If you are not attached you have nothing to lose. You are a free man. Kitty watched him. He tapped his head. Why else am I still alive? Listen, said Kitty, putting down knife and fork, the war is over. Why can't you understand? The war is over? he asked. Are you sure? One must travel light, be able to

flee at a moment's notice. But what could happen? asked
Kitty. Ho ho, he cried. Many things. His white wavy hair
stood out from his head. A woman is like a honeypot. Easy
to fall into, hard to climb out of. He lapped up the spreading yellow yolk with his bread. Kitty leaned forward. But
Joseph, we wake up and go to bed together. We eat together, drink together, talk together, make love together.
Isn't that attachment? Isn't that love? He was silent for a
moment, mopping at his mouth with his handkerchief.
Have I told you the one about the rabbi and the goats?
Kitty sighed and picking up her knife and fork, cut her egg
into small squares. No? he prompted. Would you like to
hear it? Kitty shook her head. No. I'm tired. Then, he said
with a wink, I will take you straight to bed. What do you
think of that my baby? We'll do it seated and kneeling and
crouching and crawling. Backwards and forwards. Not
now, replied Kitty pushing her plate away. He watched
her. Don't be sad darling. That's the way I am. I'm not cut
out for attachments. That's for other people. You for in-
stance. Marry a nice young man with a good position at
the bank who will get you pregnant within nine months of
the wedding day. You don't mean that, said Kitty, her face
hot. No, he agreed, I don't. The truth is I am becoming too
fond of you. He unstuck the top of his little metal box and
began to roll a cigarette. Couldn't you try? asked Kitty. Oh

sweetheart. If only it were as easy as that. I know you love me, said Kitty. The tobacco scattered over the thin white paper. Come darling, he said briskly, licking it closed, let's drown our sorrows in lust. In bed together we are never bored. Never mind about love. Kitty put down her knife. This bread is like wood, she remarked.

But that night he held her close and told her he loved her. Moonlight thin as a hair slipped in through the shutters and lit up the pores of their skin. They stayed up half the night with lovemaking and as the hours passed he told her things he had never told her before. How he needed her, how she was the light of his life. He shouted as he took her and when it was over he quoted to her from the Song of Songs. Kitty fell into a delirium, her limbs soft and pliant with love, her mouth swollen. And when she woke in the morning she turned to him full of tenderness. Everything had changed. But he was not there.

She found him at the table, showered and shaved and dressed already, full of energy as he made the coffee and defrosted a small coffee cake. Well my darling, he announced, I will soon be leaving. He pulled out a paper filter and set it carelessly in the glass pot. Sit, he said to her indicating her place. Kitty sat down at her place and pulled her kimono around her. What do you mean? she asked in confusion. It is time for me to go back to Europe. This country of yours is too new, too clean. I must get back to the steel-gray skies, the blackened stones, the history whose bones stick in my craw. If I am at home anywhere it is there. What shall I do in this place with no past? He poured the coffee through the filter. Time for me to leave. Kitty stared at him. I can't understand, she protested, her voice thick with sleep. After last night? Particularly after last night, he said forcefully. No coffee for me, said Kitty rising unsteadily. Where are you going? he asked setting down the pot. I am going to get dressed, she said. And then I am going home. I've had enough. He came after her. No need darling. I'm not leaving yet. There's still time. She turned to him angrily. Still time, cried Kitty. For what? One more story?

You silly girl, he said softly, you listen to my stories because you have none of your own. How can you say that? she cried, her cheeks flushed. I've lived too. It's not the same, he replied. Who was your grandfather? Where did he live, what did he do? Why do you ask me that now?

she said heatedly. I don't know. She paused for a moment.
I think he had a shop somewhere in Germany. And the
other one? I'm not sure. Where in Germany? She shook
her head. Was he a religious man? What about the other
one? How did they come to America? What about aunts
and uncles? What muddy villages did they flee from?
Where are the stories? he asked. What kind of Jews forget
their own stories? They didn't want to talk about it. I
asked them. Again and again. They looked away, they
changed the subject, agreed with each other that the
roast beef was particularly good that night. They asked
about school and how my piano lessons were going. She
fingered the sash of her kimono. They wanted to protect
me, maybe. Start anew. Start anew? he said with scorn.
This is the dream of a firefly, a summer moth. Kitty closed
her eyes for a moment. Never mind, darling, he murmured. I know better than you.

He circled around her as she walked, unseeing, to the
bedroom. I'm going to help you, he said. Help me? Help
you to write your book. After all, you're only a beginner.
And I'm a successful playwright. You can learn everything
you need to know from me. I will show you just how to do
it. The right way to tell the story. Kitty pulled away from

him. But it's my story. Of course it is my angel, of course it is my darling. He put his arms around her and kissed her cheek. But you can't object to a famous author giving you a few suggestions. Do you want to meet Günter Grass? Saul Bellow? I know them all. And they know me. I want to go, said Kitty, flushed, pulling away. He held on to her. You mustn't go, he said softly, mustn't leave me in the dark all alone. He gathered her up against him. Look how beautiful you are, he said. Come to me my baby, he murmured, kissing her fingers, let me climb your soft thighs, let me enter into your heart and lungs. Let me love you. She looked at herself in the small mirror that hung crookedly on the wall. I'm tired, she told him.

In the bedroom she reached for her clothes, which had lain on his chair for so long. He grabbed her arm. What's wrong with you? he wanted to know looking down at her nakedness. She shivered. I want to go. He took her in his arms. Let me go, she said, I don't want you to touch me. I won't let you go, he said forcefully. She stood stiffly in his embrace. Let me go, Joseph. You mustn't leave, he said softly. What will I do without you? He took the blouse from her hand and let it drop to the floor. He pressed his face against hers and spoke against her ear. You have no idea how I need you. You mustn't leave me. Kitty pushed him away angrily. You're the one who's leaving, she cried. He grabbed at her thick hair. What do you want me to do? he asked fiercely. Turn myself inside out for you? Where will my strength go, my resolve? How will I survive? Is that what love does? asked Kitty removing his hand from her hair. He gathered her up against him and began to kiss her face and her neck.

He sat her down and retied the sash of her kimono. Now listen to me, he said. I won't let you go. Kitty tried to get up and he pulled her down. Wait a minute. He held her arm tightly. Listen, he said harshly. I am going to change my life for you. Live as I've never lived. Shall we stand under the wedding canopy together? Side by side before the rabbi? We'll exchange a kiss, break a glass underfoot, live like other people live. What do you say darling. A happily married couple. You'll wear an apron and I'll smoke a pipe. Or shall I wear an apron and you smoke a pipe? Later we'll sit in the synagogue and dream of the roast waiting at home. We'll have seven children, three girls and four boys and be happy as anything. Would you like that? Doesn't that sound nice? The last time I asked a woman to marry me I was ten years old. Her name was Liesl Sonnenberg.

Have I told you about Liesl Sonnenberg? Joseph, said
Kitty, studying him, are you being serious? Does a Jew
like black bread with herring? he asked her. No really,
Kitty persisted. Really, murmured Joseph, as you say in
America.

He poured a stream of sugar into his coffee. We'll live like
other people, shall we? he asked animatedly. Would you
like that darling? Are you ready to throw in your lot with
a madman? Tie your future to the frayed ropes from which
I hang? He gave a short laugh. Might as well join the circus or check into the nearest madhouse. He stirred his coffee noisily, the spoon clattering against the cup. We'll go
to Vienna for our honeymoon. The beautiful and imperial
city of Vienna. The Ring, the Hofburg, Schönbrunn, pastries at Demel, Sacher torte at the Sacher. He lifted his
cup and drank. On second thought never mind all that
pompous nonsense. I'll take you to the Prater. The wonderful Prater.

When I was a child we went there every day after school.
We were forbidden to go, of course, but who could resist.

At the beginning of the Allee stood a vendor of dirty French postcards. He knew us. Come boys, he would say with a wink, I have something for you. He would take out a few postcards in black and white. You cannot imagine the excitement. In one a plump woman with soft black hair piled high on her head turned to look at us with sleepy cowlike eyes. Her bottom was as round and white as the moon. In another two women faced each other in nothing but their black stockings and little shoes. We saw their dimpled bottoms, their soft white breasts as one reached out a tentative finger to touch her friend's nipple, crowns of wildflowers in their hair. We had never imagined anything like it. We crowded around in a frenzy of yearning although we hardly knew what it was we yearned for.

We were on the best of terms with the man who bit the heads off chickens. We knew the family of midgets who tumbled together and stood in pyramids on top of each other's shoulders. And the bearded fat lady. Oh darling you cannot imagine. She was enormous. Her massive bare arms rippled, her middle was the size of a small cart. The hair on her head was as black as pitch and a black furry beard encircled her small mouth and hung down to her chest. The excitement of it all! In the shiny blue satin of her dress, just over the left breast was a small hole which she would uncover to prove she was not a fraud. But only for boys over fourteen. I couldn't wait for my fourteenth birthday. But I left Vienna too soon, damn it. I never got to see it though I dreamed of that hole for years afterwards and it took on an erotic life of its own.

In the woods beside the Prater I played doctor with Liesl Sonnenberg. We were ten. She had black curls and a little pink mouth like a cat and at first she did not want to play. I proposed marriage. I have to ask my mother, she told me. I agreed but insisted we become engaged. An engaged couple, I told her, is certainly permitted to fondle each other. She accepted that and let me put my hand inside her cotton panties. The next morning I lay in wait for her on the way to school. What did your mother say? I asked. She said, replied Liesl sadly, that I have to wait until I'm sixteen. We're still engaged, I told her that afternoon as we sat together beneath a bush. He laughed. I told her I would take her with me to Palestine. Next year, I proclaimed, we will be tilling the soil in the Holy Land. But Liesl didn't want to till the soil in Palestine. She wanted to stay in Vienna with her mother and father and keep on with her violin lessons. I'll come back for you, I promised her. When the land is tilled and I've built a little house for us. She said she would like to bring her mother along when the time came. Was putting my hand into a woman's panties ever that exciting again? I hope so, replied Kitty. His cheeks were shiny, he was smiling broadly. Kitty studied him. I thought you hated Vienna, she said at last. Hate Vienna? he asked in surprise. Why should I hate Vienna?

He jumped up and went to the cupboard. Standing on a stool to reach into the dark recesses he pulled out a Russian chapka. He stepped down, leaving the door to the cabinet open, and put on the hat above his striped dressing gown. What do you think? he asked. Do I look like a Russian general? Or like the Tsar himself? Go ahead. Tell me. Beneath the hat, he looked out at her fiercely. His high cheekbones lay in shadow, his broad chin was thrust forward, his shoulders thrown back. Kitty was silent. Well? he asked. You look, said Kitty, just like Stalin. Are you crazy? he cried pulling off the hat and throwing it down. What kind of madness is that? The anti-Semite of all anti-Semites. I didn't say you were Stalin, said Kitty mildly. I just said you looked like him. I'm not going to Vienna with you, he said angrily. I take it back, she said. You look like Nicholas, Tsar of all the Russias. He picked up his hat and brushed it off. All right, all right, he said.

He went to the refrigerator and pulled out a jar of cherries in brandy. He brought the jar to the table and unscrewed the lid. He pulled out a dark cherry dripping with liquid. The pungent scent of brandy filled the air. Have one, he offered and held it out to her. Listen my darling, he said excitedly, I'll start again. I'll write another play, we'll have a child. Would you like that? His face was flushed. A new life. Why not?

He turned the fur hat around on his fist, stroking the fur. I'm famous in Vienna, he said proudly. The mayor knows me. Did I tell you about the opening of *Sticks and Stones*? Kitty nodded. Marlene Dietrich came. God, how they loved me. He put down the hat and opened a drawer in the kitchen table. He began to rummage in the mess. Where is it? he cried. It's been stolen. The medal from the City of Vienna. I should have kept it under my pillow. Or in my shoe.

Ah, he said, here it is. He drew out a small velvet box and reverently lifted the lid. There on a bed of pale blue satin lay a gold medal. Presented to an illustrious citizen of the City of Vienna. Joseph Kruger, Playwright and Novelist. What do you think? he asked Kitty. Very shiny, she replied. He lifted the red-and-gold cross and pinned it clumsily to his striped bathrobe. It hung askew over his chest. He imitated the raucous notes of a trumpet and saluted smartly. Kitty waited. Presented to me, said Joseph, by the mayor of Vienna in a special ceremony. He was quiet for a moment, his eyes fixed on a point beyond her. On his chest, the golden points of the medal gleamed.

Slowly he unpinned the medal. Beautiful Vienna. Wonderful Vienna, he said bitterly. Where pious Jews had their beards torn out by the roots. Where my mother was ordered to kneel on the cobblestones and scrub them with a toothbrush. While the Viennese stood around with sly smiles on their faces and made obscene jokes. What fun. Better than the Prater even. He jabbed an angry finger at his temple. What kind of a madman am I? I must be the king of the idiots. He held the medal on the palm of his hand for a moment examining it. It shone as brightly as

the Emperor's crown. Those Viennese bastards, he said
quietly. He laid the medal back down in its box. Look at
that. Lying on a pale blue satin bed. Just like a corpse. He
shut the box and looked up at her. I am so very sorry my
darling, he said. But I cannot take you to Vienna.

Out the train window the snow is falling. Soft silent flakes
that drift down onto the flat ground. Where did the Austrians get the idea for their pure white eiderdowns? he
asked her once. From the snow of course. The deep soft
snow that buries Austria in forgetfulness so the Austrians
can sleep at night.

In a fenced-off field stand two horses, their dark brown winter coats flecked with snow, their rough horsehair tails
blown by the wind. They are looking expectantly ahead of
them, gauging the change in weather, listening for the wind.
In the distance stand the farm buildings, dilapidated, the
sides patched. Then red-tiled roofs, a steeple and just beyond, rows of neat white crosses. They never went to Vienna together. Years later she went with Henri. It was winter
and the city was covered in snow. She could not stop thinking of Joseph. They had taken a room at the Imperial, seen

Un Ballo in Maschera at the Opera, dined in the best restaurants, spent hours in the Kunsthistorisches Museum, ridden in an open carriage, walked through Schönbrunn. Not Joseph's Vienna at all. On the last day Kitty had suggested they go to the Prater. The Prater? asked Henri in astonishment, flakes of snow on his hat, his face red with the cold. Why go to the Prater? It's just a tawdry amusement park. You've seen *The Third Man* once too often. I want to see, said Kitty passionately, tugging at her woolen scarf, the man who bites the heads off chickens, the fat lady with a beard, the midgets, the man who sells dirty postcards. Henri laughed and brushed the snow from her hair. Darling, what in the world are you talking about?

I went back to Vienna once, Joseph told her. I went to the Prater and bought a ticket for the Big Wheel. The sky was filled with stars. I watched the gigantic wheel, glistening with lights as it turned in the night sky. I stepped into the seat and rose higher and higher above the city of Vienna. Below me lay the dark expanse of the Danube, the rooftops of Vienna, the Ring, the Hofburg, Schönbrunn. What had changed? The thing's still turning, I thought. After all that happened, it goes on. And the others. The charming Viennese. The ones who created the waltz. The ones who once stood in the Heldenplatz cheering hysterically for the new conqueror. They too were still going on, still turning as though nothing had happened, nothing had changed. I closed my eyes and grew dizzy. There was no limit to the madness of this world.

Kitty buttered a slice of bread and began to chew slowly. High up on one of the shelves stood an African woman in ebony, her breasts pointing straight out, her full lips pressed forward, her intricate wooden hair gleaming. Joseph watched her carefully, even his breathing was silent. Kitty poured herself a glass of schnapps and would not look at him. You mustn't be disappointed, said Joseph. Please darling don't be disappointed. Think how disappointed we were. Now you see it, now you don't. Whole families, whole towns. Now you see it, next thing you know they've all disappeared. Where have they gone? Only a great magician can make a whole people vanish. There far more magic is needed than to make a rabbit disappear. Kitty chewed without looking up. He reached out for her. Look what beautiful hands you have, he said smoothly. Like porcelain with those long graceful fingers. From what good fairy did you get your beautiful hands? You won't seduce me with that, said Kitty pulling her hand away. Have I told you about . . . Kitty shook her head. I don't want to hear any more.

All my lives have gone up in smoke, he told her. But you, you are still young. You have your life before you. He poured out more schnapps. There is nothing like it, he said, to give one courage, and he raised his glass to her. One may have more lives than a cat, he told her, but sooner or later even those lives run out. Kitty shrugged. You're only sixty. There's plenty of time. He laughed briefly. Is that so? Do you know they used to train dogs to run with a shot glass of schnapps on their head without spilling it. Who thinks up this insane kind of fun? It may be, he said, that when I see the leaden skies of Europe I will revive. A certain hatred of the old cobblestones will arise in me and give me energy. You do not know, he said to her, the strength that hatred brings to you. I don't care what the Nazarene and his friends had to say about love and the other cheek. That's not the way it works. Neither then. Nor now. I may even go to Vienna. Or Berlin. There the black rage will come to me and I will be ready for the next Act. You're a young girl. You know nothing of all this. No, of course not, she replied. Sweetheart, he said softly, you don't want me. I would make you miserable. Get yourself a young man. Clean and proper and rich who doesn't know what can happen in this world of ours. You don't need an old wreck like me. But never mind. You are very sweet. And wherever I am I will keep my eyes open for your book. The book which has yet to be written.

She watched him spread liverwurst thickly over his bread. A dab of liverwurst stuck to his finger. His robe had a smear of grease near the pocket. He bit off half the slice and chewed rapidly, his mouth open. For God's sakes, she said irritably, wipe your mouth. He stopped chewing. Who are you? he asked. My governess? I can't bear your bad manners, she cried heatedly. It drives me crazy. That bad? he replied. Let me tell you something. My mother taught me to wipe my mouth and say please and thank you, just like yours. Do you think I grew up in a whorehouse or on the waterfront? Not at all. But we forgot our manners. It would have been nonsensical to remember them. There were other things to think about.

The war emptied out the houses and threw everyone together like it or not. Yeshiva boys hidden in houses of debauchery, perfumed Jewish bankers squeezed into trains beside caftaned Jews from the shtetl stinking of onions. The social fabric frayed and tore. You survived or you didn't. We weren't playing the piano or attending tea parties or putting on our white gloves. I had other things to think about than please and thank you and keeping my mouth clean. That belonged to another lifetime. There were no pianos or teapots or white gloves. They had all been stolen. By birds with hard beaks and glittering eyes who had lusted for pianos and jewels and teapots in silver and gold all their lives and now they would have them— for free. Do you know how long we would have survived with your manners? Don't be such a good girl. So upright, so honest, so well mannered. Is that a way to live? Only in peacetime, in a well-to-do family, does one have the luxury of this. In a childhood where nothing at all happened beyond the falling of a leaf, the accidental overturning of a chair. How long would you have survived the war, with all your exquisite manners?

He pressed the rest of the slice into his mouth. I will tell you something else. Before the war the Dutch Jews were assimilated, accepted. They were used to tolerance. Not like the Polish Jews. So when the time came the Dutch Jews didn't know how to fight for a crust of bread in the camps. Too well mannered. Just like you. With dire consequences. Remember that the next time you put on your white gloves and dusty bonnet and give me a lecture. He mopped at his mouth and chin with his handkerchief. Kitty looked at the bent and yellowing postcards he had stuck to the wall. Why don't you get rid of those? she asked, gesturing toward them. Everything here is old and useless.

The whistle was blowing sharp, strident. The steam escaping from the battered hole. A night of yowling cats. Can't you get that? she cried. You, he replied evenly. Carefully he opened a thin sheet of paper and lay tobacco in its seam. He smoothed it with a large finger cautiously as though he were building with miniatures, rolled it tightly and licked it. She watched his broad pink tongue moving slowly like a brush. Why should I? she asked. It's your house. Oh is that how it works? he asked as he lit his rolled cigarette and watched it flame up for a moment. Is that in your etiquette book at home? Who gets the kettle? The screeching and singing of the escaping steam continued. It seemed to rise higher and higher, pouring out its fog in an angry sputtering stream. She heard the shrillness pressing against her ears, the shrieking went through her skin and bones. She put a hand to her ear. I feel like pouring it down your neck, she cried. And cream and sugar after it? he asked. He reached out a hand for her across the table. Then you'd have to lick it all off, he said softly. He smoked calmly, rounding his mouth and pressing out smoky rings. All you have to do is get up and turn it off. She crossed her arms fiercely, her face creased against the screech. I see that there's trouble in the Balkans again, he said. She looked at him with narrowed eyes. Very amusing, she replied. Amusing? he inquired. I'm talking about politics. The shrill high song was inside her head now. All you have to do is get it, he said quietly. Just get up from where you are and turn off the gas. She sat with her jaw set. It's not so very much, he went on. She could not bear the sound another second. She stared into the grain of the wood. And then at last, she got up and went to the stove and turned it off. Bravo, he said. She looked at him in fury. Sometimes, she said, I hate you. He turned and put an arm around her waist. You mustn't be so defiant, he said softly. It's only a kettle. Now pour the tea.

Out the train window she sees that the storm is over, the snow tapering off, falling lightly on the white ground in the gathering darkness. For the moment there is not a light, not a chimney, not a thatched roof to be seen. After a moment she looks down at her watch beneath the cuff of her glove. It won't be long until they reach Amsterdam.

What will you do once I leave? he asked her. Go home and write my book. Yes, he agreed. Why else have I told you so many stories. Ha, she said, because you like to hear yourself talk. Because you are in love with your past. Not only, he replied. He pulled out his white handkerchief. Are you going to make a rabbit disappear? asked Kitty. No, darling, he replied, not this time. Only myself. He watched her. Don't look so sad my angel, he said. You are better off without me. I'm not sad, said Kitty defiantly.

Kitty touched the charred edge of a cigarette burn etched in the wood. What will you do in Europe? Write another book, another play? Joseph sighed. How can a man write when he has no language. But you've already written so many plays, so many books. Then what need, asked Joseph, for another one? My language is gone, buried beneath the black earth, and every year it recedes farther and farther away. My language is Viennese, Viennese as the

Jews spoke it, soft and hard, full of irony and tenderness. In that language I am myself. How can I write properly in English, this hard unforgiving tongue of yours, without softness, without humor, without irony. This language has no resonance for me, no meaning. But I am caught between languages, in no-man's-land, an abyss of which you have no comprehension. I am a bird that cannot alight. You cannot understand that of course. You live in the language you were born with, you repeat the sounds you have always lived with. Around each word clusters a universe of sounds and smells. How can I write without the words? But you wrote six plays in English, said Kitty, and two novels. Did I? he asked wearily and mopped at the table with his handkerchief.

Do you know what it was for me to hear my son Stefan singing English nursery rhymes? I didn't know where I was. There he sat singing in his toneless child's voice and I thought why doesn't he sing the songs I sang instead of these rhymes I could barely understand. Jack Sprat? Who was Jack Sprat? And Little Miss Muffet? What kind of nonsense was that? And German? asked Kitty. German was the murderers' language. After my early plays I fled it like you flee the hangman. And then I forgot. The words drift off, the constructions fall apart, and you find there is no way back.

As the days passed he seemed to age. His movements grew heavier, his eyelids sagged, his stories grew fewer and far between. And she saw that his face was covered with perspiration which he wiped away wearily with a large white handkerchief.

He got up heavily and went to the closet. Kitty heard the soft brush of folders falling. Scheisse, he muttered and bent to pick them up. Look, he said holding out the folders to her. She had seen them so many times before. He put them down on the table. There were three folders overflowing with yellowed clippings. Not since Kafka they wrote, he told her, pressing the reviews on her. Look at this, he said, reading out loud: an imagination so vivid and inventive . . . greatest talent of the postwar years, a sensibility blacker than night. A writer like Kruger comes along once in a generation. That was the book critic of *Die Zeit.* Well? he asked her. Do you know how many prizes I've won, how many awards I've been given? How many prizes . . . He sat down heavily, his face flushed. He leaned back and closed his eyes and Kitty saw that he was old. Um Gottes willen, he said softly. Dear God.

Tell me a story, said Kitty. He opened his eyes and smiled sadly at her. I have no more stories. Yes you do, she urged him. You remember them. So, he said in sudden comprehension. You liked my stories more than you admit. More than that even, he continued, watching her. As I told you long ago, what is a Jew without his stories? If he carries nothing else with him, not even a pair of shoes or a handkerchief, he carries his stories with him. They are his house, his four walls, his ark. He pulled at his earlobe. But my stories are my stories. You must go out and get your own. Take me to bed, said Kitty softly. Oh darling, he replied, I'm tired. It seems even that is going. You mustn't give up, said Kitty. Not yet. It's too soon to give up. Too soon? he asked. How many lifetimes does it take? My poor darling, he said, you want everything to end happily. I feel like crying, said Kitty. Only I'm too sad to cry. He nodded. Good. Now you are beginning to understand.

Kitty looks out through the train window. High above in the white sky the pale moon still keeps pace with them.

The myth tells how the moon lost all her children and that is why by turns she hides all of her face, part of her face. It is a gesture of mourning, hiding oneself away like that in the night sky. She opens the second small bottle of red wine and pours it into the plastic glass. The dark red liquid moves with the movement of the train. I have to hate you, he told her toward the end, so I won't love you. What kind of madness is that? she asked. Mine, he replied. She looked into his eyes. I'm afraid when you talk like that, she said. Who isn't afraid? he asked.

On the last night they lay in each other's arms. What was there to say? Nine floors down they heard the faint sound of horns honking. He pressed his forehead against hers. Give me another minute and I will know what you are thinking. All will be transmitted. Kitty stroked his hair. You mustn't forget this bed. No, she replied. Or the eiderdown. He pulled it up over her shoulders. How warm you are, he murmured, how delicious. He kissed her face. And you mustn't forget how we lay here together in each other's arms. She didn't answer. No more stories, he whispered, not tonight. Only ours. She lay against the warmth of his chest, her legs entwined with his. We have the whole night, he told her. Sometimes, during the war, that was a lifetime. She squeezed his arm warningly. I thought you weren't going to talk about the war. I'm not.

Come darling, he murmured, let us crawl into the same skin. Let us stay here forever. No more stories, he repeated. Not tonight. He rolled over on top of her. Kitty groaned beneath him. I cannot bear to leave you, he said. That's the truth. She took his face in her hands. Never mind, darling, she said softly. He laughed briefly. You're beginning to sound like me. The last time, she said kissing him again and again. It's the last time. By the time you are my age, he said, you will have learned to bury your sadness so deep you don't even know it's there. She shifted. But you do know it's there. You just said so. She hooked her legs around his waist. Oh my darling, he murmured. Not since before the war. Have I told you . . . Yes, she said, many many times.

In the last moments, as he stood on the threshold of his apartment, he turned to her. You mustn't forget my stories. He had put on a blue shirt and brushed back his hair.

He seemed younger, lighter, excited even. Kitty stared at him. How handsome you are, she said. He straightened his shoulders and smiled at her proudly. I always was, he replied closing the door behind him. The beige walls were dingy, the hall dimly lit. She stood beside him on the darkly flowered carpeting. Joseph picked up his suitcase and slung a carry-on bag over his shoulder. Come on, he said, what's the matter, can't you move? She reached out to him. Don't forget me, Joseph, she murmured. Oh darling, he replied, beginning to move down the hall ahead of her. How could I forget you? You are tattooed on my heart. He rang for the elevator. I mustn't miss the plane, he said looking at his watch. They got into the elevator and stood together beneath the blinking fluorescent bulb. Look at your beautiful green eyes, he said to her. He took out his white handkerchief and wiped his forehead.

They went out together through the dark lobby, he carrying his battered brown leather suitcase. Kitty watched him. You look like a refugee, she whispered. What else? he replied pushing open the glass door. She felt nothing of his embrace. The taxi driver, a Sikh with a pale blue turban wrapped around his head, took his suitcase and slung it into the greasy trunk. Joseph got into the taxi. Kitty stood on the sidewalk. He rolled down the window. Why are you leaving me? whispered Kitty. He looked at her out of motionless dark eyes and shook his head slowly. The taxi started up with a lurch and Joseph leaned forward frantically. Driver, he called out, wait a minute. But already the man was honking, turning the wheel out into the traffic.

The train is coming into the Amsterdam station. Beneath the soaring iron rafters, the glass roof, the train glides noiselessly up to the barrier and comes to a halt. He was here. In November of 1938. Kitty stands and takes down her small overnight bag and puts on her gloves. The doors open and the frigid air enters. She steps out onto the station platform and hears the guttural sound of Dutch. Two girls pass arm in arm. You should have seen those Dutch girls from before the war, he told her. What a paradise. With their blue eyes and milky lips. Have I told you about Marijke? Ahead of her she sees the sign for taxis with an arrow. During the war, Joseph told her, only the Germans had gasoline, no one else. Everyone walked. Or biked. But soon the Jews could no longer bike. Or go to the park. Or to the movies. I lost my Jewish eyes and became a Dutch laborer. All this long before you were born.

His photo had appeared on the next to the last page of the paper. Henri had already left for work. He has won another literary prize, thought Kitty in her kitchen, putting down her coffee cup. My mother predicted I would win the Nobel Prize, he told her once. And I was only nine then. Kitty looked up. Out the window the sky was flat and gray. Across the square the stone ramparts of the church rose up. One tower was encased in scaffolding and for a long time she watched two men working up near the summit. And then she returned to the photo. He hadn't changed much since she had seen him all those years ago. He didn't seem to have aged. She cut a slice of bread and spread it carefully with jam. And then at last she allowed herself to stare into the dark heavy-lidded eyes. Oh Joseph, she murmured, my God.

Joseph Kruger, renowned Austrian Jewish writer, born in Vienna, died yesterday of heart failure at the age of seventy. The heart grew too weak to pump, the lungs filled with fluid, and life ceased. It seems it is possible to drown on dry land. As a child he fled from the Nazis. He was known for his surrealistic tales of the war, in which a Jewish child turns into a fish, hides in a canning factory, lives with prostitutes, and joins the circus, as well as his plays about the war, which the critics called brilliant but black as night. He wrote ten plays and three novels, received numerous prizes and awards, as well as a medal from the Austrian government. He referred to himself as an actor always playing a role, a tightrope walker balancing on a rope the width of a hair. He was married and divorced twice and had two sons, both of whom predeceased him. He will be buried in Amsterdam where he resided during the Second World War.

It was after Joseph left that she began to write. All the words that had once refused to come poured out and arranged themselves on the page. She has published three novels, moved to Paris, married. For years she has imagined that one day, in a cafe in Paris or Rome, Vienna or Amsterdam she will see him sitting at a nearby table. She will go and sit down beside him. He will turn to her and smile slyly. Well my darling, back so soon? And they will take up where they left off. He would have laughed at the notion. A chance meeting in a cafe? A happy ending? What kind of sentimental schmaltz is that? Have I taught you nothing at all, my angel?

Kitty stands for a moment beneath the vaulted glass roof, her breath icy, her cheeks stiff with cold. The war has been over for fifty years. Before her is the flutter of wings and a pigeon swoops down to the platform, his gray head moving convulsively. She claps her hands and he rises quickly, his iridescent molten wings flapping. Kitty looks up. Packed tightly together along the metal ribs of the roof, the other pigeons have already tucked their heads down in sleep. Through the glass, high above, the sky is dark, the snow has stopped.

War Story

QUESTIONS FOR DISCUSSION

1. "Does life begin again? Does the past float off like a barge down a fog-shrouded river? Please . . . we all carry our pasts strapped on our backs," Joseph tells Kitty in the midst of their affair (p. 35). How is their relationship shaped by Joseph's past? By Kitty's? Which elements of each character's past draw them together? Which ones divide them?

2. Kitty recalls her affair with Joseph years after it has occurred. Joseph reveals his childhood to Kitty after a half-century has elapsed. Are they reliable narrators in this regard? Why or why not? Discuss the ways in which the act of remembering is central to the novel.

3. Discuss ways in which food and drink are a form of erotic currency between Kitty and Joseph. What does the storing and sharing of food symbolize to Joseph? How do his offerings both please and repel her?

4. "You listen to my stories because you have none of your own," Joseph tells Kitty (p. 141). Is this true? Why or why not? How does the refusal of Kitty's family to discuss their history compare to Joseph's constant stream of stories? Why were Joseph's own attempts at forgetting unsuccessful (p. 73)?

5. What does Joseph mean when he chides Kitty to "be a good Jew" (p. 34)? Compare Kitty's discussion of her Jewish identity (p. 37) to their discussion of God (pp. 60–61) and to Joseph's monologue about Jewish life in Nazi Europe (p. 133). What role has Judaism played in each of their lives?

6. The sexual energy between Joseph and Kitty manifests itself almost immediately. What is the basis for Kitty's attraction to Joseph? What about his attraction to her? Does age play a role? Do you think their physical relationship deepens their understanding of one another or substitutes for what they cannot share? Discuss.

7. Why are Kitty's manners—and Joseph's lack thereof—significant to the story? Is Kitty's behavior on the train (p. 118) a response to Joseph's earlier admonition: "Don't be such a good girl . . . Is that a way to live?" Why or why not? Why does Joseph insist on disregarding social mores? What do "good manners" mean to him?

8. "How can I write without the words?" Joseph moans near the end of the novel (p. 159), despite his prolific career. What does he believe he has lost? Discuss the role of language in the novel. How is Kitty's voice affected by her relationship with Joseph?

9. Why does Joseph leave Kitty? Do you think he ends their affair because he does not love her? What does he mean when he says, "This country of yours is too new, too clean." (p. 110)? Why does she choose to attend his funeral so many years later?